Calvin
and the Great Tensas River Bottom

*Happy Birthday Todd...
Best wishes to you and yours—
Ronnie Wells*

Written and Illustrated

By

Ronnie Wells

ISBN 978-1-64140-860-8 (paperback)
ISBN 978-1-64140-862-2 (hardcover)
ISBN 978-1-64140-861-5 (digital)

Copyright © 2018 by Ronnie Wells

All rights reserved. No part of this publication may be reproduced, distributed, or transmitted in any form or by any means, including photocopying, recording, or other electronic or mechanical methods without the prior written permission of the publisher. For permission requests, solicit the publisher via the address below.

Christian Faith Publishing, Inc.
832 Park Avenue
Meadville, PA 16335
www.christianfaithpublishing.com

Printed in the United States of America

Dedication

Our eldest grandson Mason William McCabe, who over five years constantly asked when I was going to finish Calvin.

Introduction

This is a fantasy about Calvin, an eleven-year-old boy, and his big dog surviving in the Great Tensas River Bottom. He has suffered many hardships, having lost both parents and his best friend. He and his five-year-old sister live in a foster home. Thinking the only way she would ever have parents of her own was for him to break his promise and let them be separated, he had come to the conclusion he was too old to be adopted. They always wanted the cute little girl, but not him. The only way to find peace and have his little sister adopted was for him to leave the foster home and live by himself in this magical swamp. In so doing, he learns about himself and those depending on him. He also forms an unlikely friendship with an old man who fishes the Tensas River for a living. The year is 1950.

*****

I grew up in Jackson Parish, Louisiana, approximately one hundred miles from Tensas Parish. For many years, my grandparents, Otis and Mattie Smith, ran an old grocery story/gas station near the Tensas River. Their youngest son, Harmon "Hoss" Smith, and his wife, Carolyn, tore the old building down in the sixties and built a more modern structure. After their deaths, it was closed for good. As a kid, I was privileged to spend time at both locations, hunting and fishing the swamps and rivers in both parishes.

This is a fictional story, some geographical descriptions of the locations may not be accurate and I have included a few plants, nuts, and fruits which may not actually exist in the Tensas Bottom, but do exist in close proximity. Even though the story is fiction, I recount several actual events which took place there. I don't pretend to be an authority on this area, but I chose this location for the story which I have been formalizing in my mind for several years. Growing up, my grandfather and I spent a great amount of time fishing the banks of the Tensas. It left a profound impression on me. I never tired of listening to his many tales of mystery and survival in this moss-laden marshland. I also knew this dark foreboding landscape could be perfectly illustrated without the use of color. Several of the drawings were done from photos I made on a float trip down the Tensas River about five years ago. My grandfather's old store is the hub for the adventure.

It is my hope the reader comes to know and love Calvin, Truman, and Miss Penny.

CHAPTER 1

Broken Promise

Standing chest deep in the river, cold and muddy, he ripped off an overall strap and hung it on the cypress log.

Skipping across a barren field, a March breeze picked up a faint whiff of cotton poison and slithered into the partially opened window next to Calvin Young's bed. From the second-floor window, there was barely enough light to see the grove of cypress trees about three miles away. The big trees lined the Tensas, creating a dark silhouette against the evening sky.

It was a cold night. With the exception of his high-top leather shoes and coat, Calvin was fully dressed under the covers. He reached for an old cigar box on the foot of the bed and took from it his most-prized possession, a gold pocket watch.

Calvin's dad, Henry Young, was only a baby when his mother died and his father had disappeared under mysterious circumstances. Calvin's dad had no memory of his Indian father or his white mother.

It is said Calvin's grandfather Hawk Young placed the watch around his baby son's neck before he vanished. This watch was the only connection that Calvin's dad had with his family. He instructed his wife to give their son Calvin the watch if he didn't return from the war.

The room was dark. Calvin rubbed his fingers over the etched name on the back: "Hawk Young." He put the watch back into the box, placed it on the foot of the bed, and pulled his quilt up to his nose. In the dim light, Calvin stared at the underneath side of the bunk above him, rehearsing his plan for the hundredth time.

He shared the second-floor room with seven other boys at the Pooles' foster home. Born December 24, 1939, eleven-year-old Calvin was the oldest. Across the hall, his five-year-old sister, Emily Mae, shared a room with six other girls. Even though the Pooles had no children of their own, they were compassionate folks and opened their home to abandoned or orphaned children.

Mr. Poole's heart attack triggered the most important decision of Calvin's life. When Mrs. Poole took all the kids to the hospital to see Mr. Poole one last time before he passed away, Calvin refused to go. Mr. Poole died on the twelfth of January, and Calvin's world changed forever.

Calvin never cared much for school, even though he was smart and made good grades. He was one of the better athletes in his class but didn't care much for sports. He thought they were a waste of time. He had endured many difficult experiences for an eleven-year-old. Walker Poole had been his best friend and mentor. He decided it would be better for him not to get close to people; they either left or died.

With the death of Walker Poole, there was talk of the kids being placed with other foster parents. Mrs. Poole wasn't sure she would be able to take care of the children by herself. There was a renewed effort to find homes for them. Mrs. Poole arranged for interviews with several families who were interested in adopting some of the children. Calvin had been through this before; they always wanted the cute little girl. Emily Mae was certainly that, and Calvin was too old.

Emily Mae was introduced to a very nice couple from Monroe. She liked them immediately and they her. How could they not like adorable Emily Mae with her blond curls and dimpled cheeks!

Calvin, on the other hand, was a different story! The last thing he wanted was the couple to feel obligated to take him. And he had no intention of being adopted. He made sure his first impression would be his last.

As he hoped and expected, the couple showed no interest in him. Calvin realized he needed to help Emily Mae have the family she so desperately wanted. To do this, he had to break the promise he had made—the promise to never let them be separated.

He watched as the sun melted into the dark wilderness known as the Tensas River Bottom. Calvin tried to focus on the task ahead. He was terrified and exhilarated at the same time. His mind was made up. He had to go!

Closing his eyes, Calvin whispered the prayer his mother had taught him, hoping for reassurance of his decision and sleep. He got neither.

Henry Young, Calvin's father, was listed as missing in action in World War II. They were told he was wounded somewhere in Dutch New Guinea. Calvin had no earthly idea where that was. He held to the hope that his father was still alive because his mother had always said that he was and that he would one day return to them.

Calvin's dad was the son of a full-blooded Indian from the Alabama and Coushatta tribes. He was named Young Hawk. He had left the Big Thicket reservation, east of the Trinity River in Texas, and had come back to Louisiana, where some of his family was living.

Calvin knew very little about his Indian ancestry, because his dad was a baby when his mother died and his Indian grandfather disappeared. The only thing his mother could tell him was his Indian grandfather left the reservation in East Texas and went back to Louisiana.

The young Indian boy showed up at a big cotton farmer's house one day, requesting work of any kind. He was hired and moved into a shed in back of the main house. He quickly displayed skills and knowledge of farming.

The handsome young man was invited by the owner and his family for dinner from time to time. It was on these occasions that one of the families' daughters caught his eye. They fell in love, but her parents weren't excited about her marrying an Indian by the name of Young Hawk. Calvin's grandfather did everything possible to gain their favor. He even changed his name from Young Hawk to Hawk Young, thinking this might make it easier for her parents and everyone else to accept him. It would be a decision that would haunt him the rest of his life.

Calvin never knew either of his grandparents. His grandmother died, and his grandfather had disappeared and was thought to be dead, when his dad was just a baby. Calvin always identified with his one-quarter Indian heritage. Whenever he played cowboys and Indians with the other boys, he always wanted to be the Indian.

Calvin's mother's family were immigrants from the Netherlands, having the light skin and blond hair characteristic of the Nordic race. Calvin and his little sister favored her more than their dark-complected father. Still in Calvin's mind, he loved the fact he was part Indian.

His mother became pregnant just before his dad was sent overseas. Together, they waited for the return of his father. Her pregnancy with Emily Mae was a very difficult one and left her very sick and weak. Calvin assumed the responsibility of caring for his ailing mom and was forced to grow up much too soon. This caused him to be more serious than most boys his age.

She died shortly after giving birth to his sister. As she lay on her deathbed, she made Calvin promise never to stop hoping and praying for his father's return. She also made him promise to take care of his little sister and not to grieve for her after she was gone. She assured him they would see each other again in heaven. Too young to understand such things, all Calvin wanted was an escape from the pain and suffering he had seen his mother endure.

Calvin was prepared to hate the Pooles' foster home when he and his sister arrived. Calvin had lost both parents, and any optimism he might have had was lost with them.

He was, however, pleasantly surprised to find in this new home a person he could count on and relate to. Walker Poole became the most influential person in his early life; he only had a few memories of his father, and those of his mother were colored with her being ill.

Foster parents were required to give the children in their care, food, shelter, and a caring environment. They were not required to love them as their own. Mrs. Poole was very good at providing just that, and the children knew they would get nothing more. She was a practical person and knew that, one day, some or all may be adopted. She refused to allow herself to get too attached lest her heart be broken if and when they left.

Walker Poole, on the other hand, was not that practical. Though it was never verbally expressed, Calvin grew to love him, and he knew Mr. Poole loved him in return. Mr. Poole proved his love to Calvin by sharing with him the most precious gift a person could: his time. As it turned out, time was the one thing he had very little of. Mr. Poole had a heart problem and knew his days were probably short. He gave Calvin all he had left.

One reason Mr. Poole had such an affection for Calvin was he had been friends with Calvin's father. They had tried to enlist in the army together, and Mr. Poole was a bit older than him. Walker Poole was refused entry into the army because of his age and health, while Calvin's father was accepted. This friendship inspired Mr. Poole to be even more concerned for the boy's welfare. He hoped his friend would one day return and that his two children would have their father again. But until that happened, he would provide as much support as he could. He wanted to share his love and respect for nature with Calvin.

Math and other boring subjects were touched lightly when Mr. Poole would substitute teach for Calvin's class at school. He would discuss the things he was most interested in: nature, wildlife, and Native Americans and their survival skills. The kids knew he had a love for the works of Henry David Thoreau, especially *Walden Pond*. The other topic he liked to expound on was President Theodore Roosevelt.

Mr. Poole's grandfather had actually accompanied the president on a bear hunt. Walker's grandfather and many of the old-timers in and around this part of Louisiana never forgave Teddy, as he was affectionately called, for giving Mississippi part of the Tensas wilderness.

In 1902, the president came to Mississippi to settle a land dispute between Mississippi and Louisiana. While he was in the area, he decided to do a little bear hunting in the Tensas wilderness. There have been different accounts of the hunt, but Mr. Poole insisted that his story was the one that actually happened.

This illustration was done from a photo I made on a float trip down the Tensas.

The guides had not been successful in their fair chase bear hunt for President Roosevelt. They were desperate for Teddy to get a bear. One of the guides decided to make sure the president would be able to collect a trophy, so he tied a bear to a tree. When the president saw this, he refused to shoot a defenseless young bear.

This episode reached the *Washington Post*. A political cartoonist decided to draw a cartoon, depicting the settling of the land dispute and the bear hunt. The first cartoon was of a vicious bear after it had just attacked a dog. This vicious bear was later changed to a cute little bear. In the second cartoon, he called it "Teddy's bear."

An enterprising toy maker and his wife, from Pennsylvania, made stuffed toys. After seeing the cartoon, they contacted the president and asked for permission to use his name for a cute little stuffed bear they had made having been inspired by the president's bear hunt in Mississippi. It was granted, and within a short time, it became a popular children's toy. Kids all over the country were now sleeping with their cuddly little "teddy bears"!

Mr. Poole would tell the story over and over. He admired the president very much and pointed out that he was both a hunter and a conservationist. He did, however, always bitterly complain that the president gave Mississippi part of his beloved Tensas River Bottom.

The main reason he forgave the president was, after the unsuccessful 1902 hunt, the president said he would return one day to the southland for another bear hunt. He wanted to go on a traditional cane break hunt in the Tensas Bottom, on horseback, with dogs.

In 1907, the president returned to Tallulah for a thirteen-day dawn-to-dusk bear hunt. The president and his party were guided by several legendary bear hunters. Among them Holt Collier, the greatest bear hunter in the south, who was also a one time slave and Confederate soldier and Mr. Poole's grandfather, a well-known authority on the Tensas wilderness.

On the hunt, the president reported they took three bears, six deer, one turkey, one duck, one possum, and one wildcat. He claimed they ate everything but the wildcat. A reporter asked how the possum tasted. The president reportedly replied, "It was the best meal they had, with the exception of the bear liver." The kids would always laugh at that point, even though they had heard the story many times.

Calvin was always proud when Mr. Poole substituted. All the kids in his class enjoyed hearing his stories. They would ask, "When is yuh daddy goin' ta substitute again?" Calvin knew he wasn't his daddy, but it was nice to hear them say it.

Mr. Poole also had a great knowledge of "the early people," as he referred to them, and their ability to survive off the land. Knowing Calvin's grandfather was from the Alabama-Coushatta tribes made him even more dedicated in teaching the boys in his foster home about their ways. Surviving in the wilderness was fascinating to him, and he shared it with anyone who would listen.

Mr. Poole would spend hours teaching the boys survival skills. Long after the others would lose interest and run off to play, Calvin and Mr. Poole would practice making fire with a bow and soaking acorns to remove the poison. They would grind them between rocks to make meal, then cook Johnny Cakes over the fire, a common food for Native Americans.

They took walks through the swamps. Mr. Poole would point out eatable plants and insects most people wouldn't consider food. Calvin was made to understand that if a person was starving, he would eat just about anything. But he decided that there were some things he would resist until he was at that point.

Mr. Poole would test Calvin's sense of direction by taking him to unknown woods and see if he could help find their way back home. Though "the early people" didn't have compasses or maps, they were never lost. From looking for moss growing on the north side of trees to finding the North Star at night, Calvin was an eager student and never tired of their survival games.

Like all the others Calvin had loved, Walker Poole would leave him. His heart was weak, and many times while out on excursions, he would have to sit down on a log and rest. Calvin was concerned, but Mr. Poole insisted, "I'm a little worn out. Don't you worry about me." At the young age of fifty-two, Walker Poole vanished like a vapor with the rising sun.

CHAPTER 2

Leaving Home

It was time. Calvin slipped out from under the covers and grabbed his shoes. He placed them on his bed, along with his cigar box. He rolled these up in the quilt, threw it out the opened window, and crawled out. He hung by his fingertips on the ledge until he was vertical. Then, as quiet as a cat burglar, he dropped to the ground.

He grabbed his bundle and, in the dark, made it across the backyard to the shed where he had placed the canvas roll and tow sack, with everything he had collected for his elopement.

Calvin unrolled the canvas, placed the quilt inside, and rolled it up again. He tied the canvas roll with a short rope, looped it over his shoulder, and grabbed the tow sack. Now the challenge was to get down the long driveway without being seen.

The ground was cold to Calvin's bare feet, but shoes would just slow him down. He didn't want to take time to put them on. With the gear strapped to his body, he ran as best he could, dodging water holes from the night's rain. Calvin planned to go only a short distance, find a good hiding place on the side of the road, and wait until the sun came up.

There was no reason to hurry. It was Sunday, and the store would be closed. He would just hang around near the store until Monday morning, when Mrs. Mattie Smith opened. This would be tricky, because she knew everyone and everyone knew her. The moment Calvin showed up by himself on a school day, the questions would be flying right and left.

He tried to imagine how the conversation might go, in order to come up with the right responses without telling too many lies. Calvin wasn't very good at lying and seemed to get caught every time he tried. There were no other options, so he figured he would just wing it and hope for the best. He knew, one way or the other, he had to get his supplies. As a last resort, he would hand her the list; and once everything was bagged, he would throw his money on the counter, grab them, and run as fast as he could for the door. Mrs. Smith was a little chubby, and there was no way she could catch him. By the time she could contact Mrs. Poole, he would be long gone!

Calvin found a good spot to spread the canvas on the wet ground. He put his shoes on without socks, then lay down, using his rolled-up quilt for a pillow. He was glad he had his coat on. It always seemed the coldest just before sunrise.

He suddenly became aware of this moment in time. Lying there looking up at the great void sprinkled with countless stars, he was transfixed as he watched them slowly fading away. The sun was still hiding behind the dark horizon, but the sky was now giving way to a pink glow. The boy felt small and insignificant. It was so quiet he could hear his own heartbeat. He was truly alone and realized he would be that way perhaps forever. All at once, Calvin was overwhelmed with every emotion possible, from the highest elation to an indescribable sadness. Feeling sorry for himself wasn't a habit, but then he had never run away from home before.

"What if I never see my little sister again?" he muttered to himself. "I had ta leave, or she won't go with thu couple from Monroe. What if she forgets me? She won't understand why I had ta leave. Maybe I did thu wrong thing. What if I can't survive in thu Tensas Bottom?"

Calvin's head and emotions were spinning like crazy. He was second-guessing himself. He tried to pretend he wasn't scared, but down deep, he knew he was terrified. This was the first time he had admitted it to himself. Maybe it was good, he thought, to accept that there was plenty to be scarred about. He needed to get his emotions under control and regain the confidence that enabled him to get to this point.

He tried to imagine the kid's reaction at school when he didn't show up. This amused him and took his mind off the more serious consequences, like breaking his promise to Emily Mae.

Reality had begun to set in. He knew this thinking had to stop if he wanted to survive alone in the wilderness. From now on, Calvin Young would no longer be able to think like a typical eleven-year-old white boy; he would think and act like a young Indian brave. This was the vow he made to himself in the predawn light.

It was light enough to see. He threw his roll over his shoulder, picked up the tow sack, and jumped the ditch.

The road was still wet, and there were a few puddles to avoid on the way to the old store.

Calvin had only walked a few yards, when the silence of the morning was broken by the sound of little bare feet splattering on the wet ground. When he turned, his heart sank. There was his diminutive blond-haired sister, in her white cotton gown, running as fast as her little short legs would allow. She was screaming, "Calvin, stop! Wait for me! Where are yuh going? Please wait for me!" This was the one thing he had hoped to avoid. He knew she would never agree to him leaving. This would be the hardest test of his life. Somehow he would have to convince Emily Mae that he no longer wanted to take care of her. She needed to go back without him and start a new life with adoptive parents.

He held up his hand and, with as much force as he could muster up, hollered, "NO! STOP! Emily Mae, don't come any closer. Yuh can't come with me! Yuh have ta go back! I don't want'uh take care of yuh anymore! You'll be adopted by some nice people, and nobody will adopt me 'cause I'm too old. And, besides, I don't want'uh be." He had never before talked to her like that. The tone of his voice scared Emily Mae.

Shocked and cold, her little body started trembling. She dropped her head, clasped her hands in front, and pleaded, "Calvin, yuh promised yuh would never leave me, and I don't want new parents without yuh." Tears were now flowing uncontrollably. "Calvin, please come back! Where are yuh going? Let me come too! I won't be any trouble!"

She started toward him with outreached arms, when he shouted even louder, "I told yuh ta go back!" Calvin dropped the tow sack, reaching down he picked up a big clod of black wet dirt and threw it at her bare feet. It broke apart and splattered on her little white cotton nightgown. She gasped at the black spots all over the hem of her gown, then covered her face with both hands, turned, and ran back toward the house.

Calvin wanted desperately to comfort her, but it was done. He whispered over and over to himself, "I'm sorry." He watched her disappear around the corner and up the drive, to the old clapboard house. Spinning around, Calvin picked up the tow sack and ran in the opposite direction. Hot tears burned his face. That was the first time he could ever remember crying; not even when his mother and Mr. Poole died.

The tears blinded him, causing him to stumble and fall facedown on the cold wet ground. He lay there sobbing until there was nothing left. All was quiet. He couldn't move. The unspeakable hurt he had caused to the one person he loved the most was too much to bear. The image of his little sister's face after telling her he was tired of taking care of her wouldn't go away. If he just lay there long enough, perhaps it would.

It seemed time stood still. He heard a rooster crow, then a dog barking in the distance. Still he lay there. His head was buried in the fold of his arm. More time passed; still he didn't move. Then what felt like a hot wet tongue slurped across his ear.

Startled, he flipped over on his elbows and found himself staring up at a dog with a head the size of a small pony. The dog sat back on his haunches, then leaned forward until their noses were almost touching. The large head possessed one dark eye and one startlingly light-blue eye, tucked under a heavy brow.

Chapter 3

The Big Dog

They just looked at each other for a while. Calvin thought he was in the presence of a creature from another planet. The sheer size and aloofness of this canine made Calvin a bit uncomfortable. He had heard you shouldn't look an animal in the eye, because it was a sign of aggression. That was the last thing he wanted to do. But in this case, he couldn't avoid it.

The overgrown dog seemed not so impressed with the pint-size human. Either, bored with the encounter or distracted by the scent of a varmint, he sniffed the air and trotted off to explore. Calvin was in awe of this beautiful animal. He moved and carried himself like royalty. He was also totally oblivious of Calvin. Most of the stray dogs Calvin had come in contact with either wanted to lick him to death or bite him. But none had ever ignored him.

Calvin really didn't know how to react to his cavalier attitude toward him, but he began hoping that perhaps this dog was going his way. He remembered he had packed a sausage biscuit in his coat pocket. The way to any dog's heart is through his stomach, thought Calvin.

He took the sandwich and broke off a small morsel. Then, putting two fingers to the corners of his mouth, he gave a sharp whistle. The big dog raised his head and casually looked in his direction. Calvin held up the piece so he could see and smell the treat and then pitched it underhanded toward the dog. *That proves my theory*, thought Calvin, *no matter how proud you are, if you are a dog, you will still eat food off the ground when given the opportunity.*

Calvin looked at the biscuit sandwich. He was starving after the morning he had, but the thought of the dog's companionship trumped his hunger at the moment. He knew he belonged to someone; he had to. A great dog like that couldn't be a stray. If only he would walk with him to the store, it would make him feel so much better.

He wondered if he could make the biscuit last three miles. "Hey, big boy, would you like to go on adventure with me?" Calvin laughed, patting the dog's head for the first time. The dog was still sniffing the ground, looking for another taste of biscuit.

For the first time since Calvin left that morning, he began to relax a bit and enjoy this new companion. Having the big dog there was a distraction from what had just taken place. He was thankful for that, but he knew the dog could suddenly decide to go home, and he would be alone again.

"Wonder why you have no collar," he thought. "Maybe you ran away from home too!"

Calvin picked up his gear, and they both headed west toward the Smith store. The big dog took the lead but would turn back or wait for Calvin if he had gotten too far ahead. This thrilled Calvin. Occasionally, he would give the dog a bite of the sausage biscuit, pat him on the head, and take a nibble himself. *For uh eleven-year-old boy that had such uh horrible morning, this ain't half bad*, he thought.

The sun was warming things up, so he stopped to take his coat off. He laid his gear down and had gotten one arm out, when he heard a vehicle coming. He grabbed the canvas roll with one hand and hung the looped rope of the tow sack around the dog's neck, and they both jumped the ditch.

There was a row of willow saplings on the backside of the ditch. Ducking behind them, Calvin held the rope around the dog's neck until the truck passed. He knew the folks in the truck. They were headed to the old Midway Baptist Church. It was good they didn't see him.

The big dog hunkered down beside Calvin and seemed to anticipate his wishes. Calvin found himself getting too attached. Once again, he knew this was a mistake. At some point, he would have to give him up.

They hopped back across the ditch, and he adjusted the sack on the dog's back. Calvin tied his coat around his waist, picked up the canvas roll, and hung it over his shoulder; and they continued their walk. It was important to stay close to the ditch so if they heard a vehicle, they could be off the road in a flash.

Calvin was hungry. He could tell by the sun it was already past noon, but it would be Monday morning before he could buy food at the store.

The sandwich was all gone. He wished he had brought more food to start with, but the most important thing now was to get to the store without being seen. He was pretty sure Emily Mae wouldn't say where he was going, but even if she did, it wouldn't matter. Once he got to the swamp, they would never find him even if anyone actually looked. He knew the sheriff would make some half-hearted attempt, but didn't think they would make a big fuss about a missing eleven-year-old orphan.

There were a few dew berries along the road's edge. He nibbled on them, knowing they would have to do for now. Calvin had eighteen dollars and some change in his pocket. This, his life savings, would purchase the list of items he would need from the store.

The tow sack contained everything he had collected over the past several months. Calvin realized the most important thing he had going for him that would possibly allow him to survive in the swamp was not in the sack. It was the survival skills he had learned from Mr. Poole. He would now rely on Mr. Poole's instructions, most of which he had never actually had to put to use other than in theory.

The pair made their way west with little interruption. It was, after all, a Sunday afternoon; and most folks were home with their families.

Calvin loved the huge live oak trees that lined the road leading up to the old store. The Smith store was a welcome sight to all. It was an oasis in the desert for the weary traveler. Their motto claimed, "If we don't have it, you don't need it." From groceries to farming tools, from ice cream to night crawlers, the Smith store had it all.

He loved everything about this place. The trees were massive with their limbs forming an arch over the road and creating shade in the summer and protection from the cold winds in winter. They were adorned with gray Spanish moss, which draped their limbs like old men's beards. The arch provided a formal entrance to the faded clapboard store. The Coca-Cola sign on the east wall had faded along with the clapboard, giving it the look of a Norman Rockwell painting.

He and Mr. Poole would always stop and get fish bait and snacks on the way to the river. There was a little soda counter in the back, where Mr. Poole bought Calvin his first ice cream cone shortly after he came to the foster home.

He would never forget that hot summer. Mr. Poole told him he had to eat it fast because it would melt. It was the best thing he had ever tasted. The idea he had to finish in a hurry was offensive to him. Calvin had carefully managed to lick it down to the cone, but in the process, he had cream dripping down both arms onto his shirt and pants. His hands were covered with the white sticky mess; he panicked and threw the whole thing on the counter.

Mr. Poole wasn't able to contain his laughter. "Calvin my boy," he said, "you just threw away the best part." He took the cone and held the end toward Calvin's mouth. "Now take a bite of this." He was right; there was something about the last bit of ice cream, trapped in the bottom of the cone that made it indescribably good. Thinking back about the good times with Mr. Poole made Calvin feel like an old man at the age of eleven.

The boy and the dog arrived at the corner of the now barren cotton field. It stretched over a mile along the gravel road and all the way to the store. Only an old rickety picket fence separated the store from the cotton field.

The sun was warming things up. He found a shade and decided to lie on the ground for a while to rest his back against the sack. There was nothing else to do until the store opened. Calvin realized he was under the old live oak tree where, year after year, wagons packed with cotton pickers would gather before daylight. The cotton scales were still hanging on a limb above his head. Every fall, there would be entire families of blacks and poor whites waiting with cotton sacks in hand for enough light to start picking.

A lot of the larger cotton farmers were now using mechanical pickers, but they were more expensive and not as thorough as handpicking. Most of the smaller farmers still used pickers because they couldn't afford the extra expense or waste.

Just last September, most of the kids from the foster home, including him and Emily Mae, had their cotton weighed on those scales. The foster kids wanted to pick cotton because it would give them a little spending money for the carnival, which always came to town in September.

The going rate for cotton pickers was two to five cents a pound. They would pick every day until the field was completely picked. The cotton was then dumped into big wagons, with high wooden sides and hauled to the gin. It took about eight or nine hundred pounds of picked cotton to make a bail, depending on how much moisture it contained and how clean it was picked.

Picking cotton was hard work for little pay but didn't require a lot of skill, and most anyone could do it. It was a source of pride for kids to pick cotton and help contribute to the family's income. But, unlike the kids from the foster home, some had no choice. Regardless, those who picked cotton gained a work ethic that served them well the rest of their lives.

This was the first time for Emily Mae. She was so little she couldn't pull a regular cotton sack. Mrs. Poole made her one from a twenty-five-pound flower sack. She was as proud as anyone could be when they hung her little sack on the scale. It was so light it wouldn't actually weigh. The farmer would just empty her cotton in the wagon and put a dollar by her name.

The pickers would bring their dinner, which was usually a biscuit with sausage, a baked sweet potato, or whatever they had. All the pickers would sit under the shade provided by the wonderful old tree, eat their dinner, and rest for a while. The farmer would provide water in a large bucket with a dipper. Then without a word, the adults would slowly get up, put the cotton sack strap over their shoulder, and head for their row. The kids would follow.

Cotton was grown in large fields with varied terrain. The low areas would produce much taller cotton because it held the most moisture. There were no toilets available. If one needed to use the facilities, they would have to hold it until they made it to the high cotton. So the term being in "high cotton" denoted something desirable. The term is still used today, but most folks don't know why.

Once that field was picked, that was all the cotton picking for the foster kids, but the other pickers would go to the next field and start over again.

The reminiscing was interrupted when he noticed the dog had headed off in the direction of the store. Calvin had taken the sack off the dogs back so he could rest. Now that he was untethered, he was in a dead run, straight for the store.

Calvin stood and made a half-hearted attempt to call him back, but he didn't even know his name. He grabbed his things and tried to run after him, but with everything he had to carry, he could barely jog. He was desperate not to let him out of sight.

When the dog got to the store, he never slowed down and ran around to the back steps. Calvin was close enough now to see him clearly, as he scratched on the back screen door. The boy was surprised when the door opened and the dog ran in like that was something he had done before.

However, the door wasn't opened by either of the Smiths. He couldn't believe his eyes; the person who opened the door was like no one he had ever seen. It had been a little cool for March, but this guy was wearing a long black overcoat, a big black cowboy hat, and white cotton gloves. The thing that topped it all off was the red bandana across his nose. He looked as though he was about to hold up the stagecoach. Calvin didn't know what to do. Was it possible he was robbing the store? Maybe he had the Smiths tied up and gagged.

Calvin had reached the old picket fence. He walked behind it until he found a couple of missing pickets. Dropping his stuff on the ground, he crawled through and ran, all hunched over to the corner of the building. He paused to catch his breath and figure out his next move.

The problem was obvious; Calvin was too short to look through the windows on the back. He would have to crawl up the steps and look through the screen door. He could hear muffled talking inside but wasn't sure if the man was talking to another person or the dog.

No matter what, he would have to see if the Smiths were all right! He counted to three, took a deep breath, and crawled on his belly to the steps. Calvin ascended the steps in the same manner; and, as he lifted his head to look, the screen door flew open and knocked Calvin for a somersault down the stairs. He sat up facing the big dog with the one pale blue eye.

From somewhere in the dark interior of the store, he heard laughter. Calvin couldn't see who was laughing, but it got louder as the person came to the back door. He was experiencing the flight impulse and was in the process of making a break for it, when he found a well-placed paw in his path, and down he went again.

"I see yuh two know each other," said the stranger, still laughing. "He likes ta do thu same thing ta me. He'll stick that big ol' paw out there an' trip me from time ta time. Guess he thinks it's funny or something. He must like yuh a lot, or he wouldn't want ta play with yuh. He's a pretty serious dog most of thu time. Don't like nobody much but me," said the man.

Calvin noticed as he spoke the bandana would puff in and out.

"Tell me, what's yuh name, young fella?"

"My name is Calvin Young," he said with a defensive tone.

"I think I've seen yuh around here before," the man said. "I remember seeing yuh with a bunch of other kids from thu foster home. You were getting stuff for uh camping trip on thu Tensas while I was doing some work for thu Smiths."

"Where's thu Smiths?" Calvin asked with a more assertive tone. "What are yuh doing here?" He was trying to read the man's face, but all he could see were dark eyes and a bit of very white pasty skin above the red bandana. He could tell the man was probably in his sixties, used to be quite tall, but now had a slight stoop to his back. Calvin relaxed a little when he thought he noticed a slight twinkle in the man's eye.

"The Smiths will be fine. Both have uh touch of thu flu. I was doing some white oak canein' on their chairs, out at their place, so they wanted me ta come over ta thu store an' get 'em some aspirin an' cough syrup. They gave me thu key to thu back door. I'll lock it back when I take 'em thu medicine. I'm staying in their ol' shed over there until I finish thu job. Then I'll be moving on. Don't stay in one place too long."

"That's my dog that ran yuh over. Sorry 'bout that. He pulls my cart." He nodded to a goat cart over by the shed that was full of white oak logs.

"If I can't find any white oak close, I have ta take it with me. He's strong as uh horse, big as one too. He can pull uh load of logs with no trouble," said the man.

Calvin finally felt relaxed enough to speak. "He's thu biggest dog I ever seen. What kind uh dog is he?" asked Calvin.

"Well, I tell yuh, I had uh old Catahoula Cur dog, an' I was doing some canein' over at that fancy plantation home, near Tallulah. They had this high-fa-lutein Great Dane. They seemed ta take uh liking ta each other. It took me two or three months ta finish thu canein' job, because they had so many chairs an' benches. So 'bout thu time we were going ta leave, she had uh litter of pups. They weren't real happy 'bout it, said if I wanted one, better get it now 'cause they were gone 'a put 'em in uh sack an' throw 'em in thu Tensas River. So there he is." He motioned in the dog's direction.

The big dog sat up and cocked his head, as though he knew he was being talked about.

"He was thu only one with a glass eye."

"Yeah, he's some kind 'a fine dog. Wish I could'uh got me one of them pups before they threw 'em in the river," said Calvin, shaking his head.

"Yep, that was uh shame, but I'll tell yuh, taking care of a dog like that's uh full-time job," the man said.

"I could do it," Calvin said under his breath. "What's yuh name? Yuh never told me," asked Calvin.

"Folks just call me thu Canein' Man because I walk all over this part of Louisiana canein' chair bottoms. I don't use cane much, though, unless they don't want oak. I use white oak 'cause it splits good. I can split it in half-inch strips, soak 'em in water, an' they'll bend like paper. They're easy to plat then and last forever too!" he said.

Calvin knew better than to talk to strangers, but for some reason, he could tell this unusual-looking person meant him no harm.

Calvin could stand it no longer; he had to ask, "Mister, why are yuh wearing that handkerchief on yuh face?"

The man stumbled for an answer but finally said, "Oh, well, uh, uh, the Smiths have thu flu, an' I didn't want ta catch it." Calvin wasn't sure about this answer but decided to let it go at that.

"Yuh don't want 'a come in here either," he said. "Thu flu's going around."

Calvin blurted out, "But I have ta come in. I got 'a get supplies!"

"Get supplies for what? Why do yuh need supplies? Where yuh going?" asked the Canein' Man.

Calvin sat there staring at the ground. He couldn't believe he was going to spill his guts to this stranger, but he felt something in common with the man whom he just met. Maybe it was the fact they both seemed to be homeless. Whatever reason, he finally said, "It's uh long story." The man sat down on the steps.

CHAPTER 4

The Gift

When Calvin finely finished, the man stood, turned his back to the boy, and wiped his eyes with the bandana.

"I should tell yuh to go back, but who am I givin' such advice? Look at thu life I live! So, instead, I'll help yuh all I can. Son, I know yuh think yuh know how ta survive in that river bottom. I'm sure thu good man at thu foster home taught yuh everything he knew, but that might not be enough. It's gone 'a be harder than yuh can imagine. Every day is different. Yuh can never know everything about that swamp. If yuh think yuh do, it'll kill yuh. Yuh just uh boy! I understand yuh think yuh have to do it for yuh little sister's sake, but maybe yuh should listen to what I have ta say first," said the Canein' Man. "I've lived there for months at uh time. There's been many grown men die in that swamp. Yuh stay here. I'll take this medicine ta thu Smiths. When I get back, I have some things ta talk ta yuh 'bout."

Once the Canein' Man returned, he told Calvin he had asked the Smiths if it would be all right to write a ticket for some supplies. They said they would take it out of what they owed him.

He talked to Calvin until the wee hours of the morning, telling him how he had lived in the Tensas River Bottom by himself, with only a dog for companionship. He tried to tell him everything he would need to know. When Calvin couldn't hold his eyes open any longer, he lay down on the ground and fell asleep.

The Canein' Man covered him with a blanket and left him there, knowing there would be many uncomfortable nights ahead. He then went about collecting everything he knew the boy would need.

When Calvin woke the next morning, he was absolutely starving. He had only eaten a few dewberries and part of a biscuit in the past twenty-four hours.

There was a smell in the air that was driving him insane. Bacon was popping in a cast-iron skillet on an open fire. Another contained cat head biscuits. He saw some blackberry jam, along with a glass of fresh milk, sitting on an upside-down apple box.

Calvin sat up and looked around, wondering where the Canein' Man and his big dog were. The back screen door flew open, and the dog cleared all four steps with one leap. He ran for Calvin, tail wagging, bouncing around the yard with a morning greeting that only a dog truly understands. Calvin reached to pet him, but the dog quickly sidestepped, wanting to tease him into a chase. He tried to grab the dog, but he was too fast for Calvin.

The Canein' Man laughed. "Yuh boys cut that foolishness out. Better save yuh energy. It's time ta eat an' be on yuh way if yuh still going ta do this." Calvin nodded his answer.

"Yuh breakfast is ready. This is thu last time somebody else will make it for yuh," the Canein' Man said as he emerged from the shed.

"I've been putting yuh supplies together like I told yuh I would last night. There's uh little tub, machete, uh shovel, hatchet with uh file, an' uh plow-line rope forty foot long, already in thu cart. Eat, an' I'll put all thu leftovers in uh sack, so yuh can take 'em with yuh," said the Canein' Man.

Calvin ate three biscuits with jam and about half a pound of bacon and then downed the glass of milk. The big dog was nosing around, waiting for scraps. Calvin was feeding him a biscuit and some of the leftover bacon when the Canein' Man said, "Don't worry 'bout him. I've already fed yuh dog this morning."

Calvin wasn't sure he'd heard right, but his heart stopped for a moment. Should he ask him to repeat what he had just said? Finally, he gathered enough courage to ask, "Did you say *my* dog?" The Canein' Man, with his bandana still covering his face, nodded yes.

Calvin wished he would take it off; he wanted to see his face. He knew there was a reason he wore it. Maybe something happened to him that made him ashamed of the way he looked. Calvin didn't care. He wanted him to know what a wonderful thing he had done for him. He felt so much gratitude toward this person but knew he wouldn't be able to express it. All he could do was grab the big dog and hug him.

"I won't be moving around so much, so yuh need the dog more than I do," said the Canein' Man. "I'll show yuh how ta hitch him ta his cart. He loves ta pull it. I guess it's just born in 'im," he said.

"Mr. Canein' Man, what's his name?" That was the first time Calvin called him that.

"Well, Calvin, he really don't have uh name. I've just been calling him Big'un most of thu time 'cause he's such uh big dog, but that's not thu right name for uh dog like him. He needs uh important name. He's uh great dog an' should have uh great name. Mr. Young, why don't yuh give him uh important name for us," he said, laughing.

Calvin thought and thought and all of a sudden shouted, "Truman! That's his name! If it's good enough for thu president, it should be good enough for him." They both laughed. "Truman, here, boy!" shouted Calvin. The big dog ignored him. "Guess he has ta get used ta it." They both laughed again.

Calvin went to the picket fence and got the canvas roll and the tow sack where he had left them overnight. He untied the short rope and unrolled the canvas with the quilt inside and emptied the contents on top. "This is everything I have."

They sat down and sorted through his collection of two khaki shirts, two pairs of overalls, one pair of khaki pants, two pairs of long handle underwear, and two pairs of socks. He also had lots of fishing line, a roll of heavy cord, hooks, lead weights, and corks. He had some cooking utensils: one pot, frying pan, fork and spoon, one metal plate, and a skinning knife in a leather sheath. Other supplies consisted of a syrup bucket, Vaseline, a bottle of iodine, baking soda, box of salt, black pepper, two boxes of kitchen matches, bunches of rags, several bars of Lava soap, for washing his one metal plate, and perhaps himself if he couldn't stand it any longer, and a canvas water bag.

Calvin opened the cigar box, which contained the eighteen dollars, along with the gold pocket watch and chain.

"This is all thu money I have. I'll give it ta yuh for all thu supplies yuh got from thu store. This is my watch. It belonged ta my dad, an' I'll give it ta yuh, for Truman."

The Canein' Man picked up the money. "That should cover thu supplies. I'll make sure thu Smiths get this. They haven't been able ta open thu store for uh few days."

He studied the watch carefully for a long time, rubbing the glass front, then turned it over, reading the name on the back, "Hawk Young." Calvin was surprised. The Canein' Man seemed to be very emotional as he shook his head. "*No*, you should always keep this! Thu dog is not for sale or trade at any price. He's uh gift."

Chapter 5

Arrival

The sun was warming the back of Calvin's neck as they approached the old wooden bridge. He filled his coat pockets with last fall's cotton balls he had picked up on the side of the road. Cotton would fall from wagons headed for the gin. His pockets were so puffed out he looked as though he had put on ten or fifteen pounds since he left. Calvin would keep them dry and rub them in the Vaseline, which contains alcohol. This would enable him to start a fire, even if everything was wet.

The sun was getting higher and hotter. Calvin had worked up a sweat with his coat on and was becoming very uncomfortable. He grabbed Truman's harness, and he came to a stop. Calvin took his coat off and laid it in the cart.

In the process, he spotted a nice straight pin oak sapling that had sprung up under the edge of the bridge. Calvin took the machete from the cart and pulled the sapling over; and, with a couple of whacks, it was separated from the stump. He trimmed the small limbs and peeled the bark off a seven-foot section. He had thoughts of turning this into a spear, but for now, it would serve as a walking stick.

Calvin couldn't help but smile to himself. He felt invincible alongside Truman, and as long as he had his dog, there was nothing he couldn't do or overcome.

The cart was full. It held ten-pound bags of flour, ten pounds of meal, Irish potatoes, a gallon of lard, five pounds of sugar, and about five pounds of bacon. Calvin knew his supplies would allow him only a little reprieve from having to live off the land every day. He also knew that from sunup to sundown, the quest for food would consume his day.

The Canein' Man said Truman would eat at least two pounds of fish per day. Truman was also good at scavenging the swamp for food. The river was full of alligator gar that could be dried or smoked whole making it easier to store a supply.

Calvin was impressed at how effortlessly Truman pulled the cart, loaded with all the supplies. It had to weigh at least seventy or eighty pounds. His original plan was to tie his gear on two long sticks and pull them like the Indians used to do. He couldn't believe his good fortune, having a dog-drawn cart. *This is the only way ta go*, thought Calvin.

Walking alongside the massive canine gave the boy new strength and confidence. Calvin had no idea how much he would need both. The fact this great dog actually belonged to him was still hard for him to comprehend.

He just couldn't keep his hands off him. Calvin was afraid he was smothering him with too much affection. The Canein' Man had said he was an independent dog and did pretty much as he pleased. Calvin worried that when he took the harness off Truman, he would run back to the Canein' Man.

They slowly crossed the wooden bridge, stopping to observe the dark murky water below. The cart wheels made a pleasant sound rolling over the uneven planks. The noise echoed over and over down the river.

Recent rain had caused the river to rise. The water level was even with the banks. He and a couple of the other boys had done cannonballs from this very spot in summers past. If he were to jump in now, he feared the current would quickly carry him downriver.

Contemplating all this, he began to formulate the scene of a horrible tragedy in his mind. He remembered Huck Finn, one of his favorite books, faking his own death. Calvin knew they would send out a search party at some point, and this plan could possibly buy him a little time. The idea was to create some speculation as to what might have happened to him. This would give him time to go deeper into the swamp and, perhaps, keep them from searching at all.

Calvin knew the high water would make fishing difficult. Fish often lose their appetite when the water is high and muddy. They only feed when they want to, not when you want them to. There were other ways to catch fish, regardless of whether they were feeding or not. Mr. Poole and the Canein' Man both suggested the use of traps. He would have to use every possible opportunity in order to exist in the Tensas swamp.

He was thankful for the staples he had. These would help him get his feet on the ground. He could focus on a few other things, rather than food, at least for a few days. This was much needed because he had plans for the cart that would require some time.

Calvin remembered a good site close to the river where he, Mr. Poole, and the boys had camped in times past. There were sandbars where he could dig a hole and let fresh clean water seep in. He knew good water is the most essential item for survival.

They crossed the bridge and looked for the road that would lead them down the bank into another world. It probably would be grown up with weeds because it was too early in the fishing season for folks to have used it much. The road was really nothing more than a trail and was always a little wet and slick. Deep ruts were cut over time, so the small wheels of the cart might present a problem.

Calvin wanted to see how Truman would handle the cart with extra weight. The big dog made the turn and braced himself to descend the embankment, knowing the cart would push him forward. *That was perfect*, thought Calvin.

They slid quietly into the wilderness. Thick greenery closed in around them on all sides. The limbs of the great bald cypress formed a canopy over their heads, making them invisible to the outside world. They were now part of the Great Tensas River Bottom, something Calvin had always dreamed about.

Pulling the cart wouldn't be an easy task. Whenever possible, they would use trails created by man or beast. Calvin knew all too well the problems the black delta mud presented. It stuck to your feet, and the further you walked, the taller you got. At some point, you would just have to stop and clean it off.

The cart wheels would need to be cleaned often. He was trying to prepare himself so he wouldn't become too discouraged with the slow pace. There were some obvious trails, which paralleled the river and a few old logging roads; they would make it easier for Truman to keep the cart moving. If there were no trails, he would have to take the path of least resistance.

Before Calvin was out of sight of the bridge, there was one last thing he had to do. He left Truman with the cart and walked a trail to a fishing spot just below the bridge. He took off his shoes and entered the water. With the bridge in sight, he waded alongside an old cypress log jutting out from the bank. The current was strong, so he held on to the log with one hand. Standing chest deep in the river, cold, and muddy, he ripped off an overall strap and hung it on the cypress log. He made sure it was in plain view of the bridge. "What uh shame. He was such uh great kid." He chuckled to himself with a little self-dedicating humor.

The smell of the swamp filled his nostrils. It was intoxicating! For some reason, he felt more at home here than anywhere on earth.

"Ain't this great, Truman? Can yuh believe it? We have it all ta ourselves! All kids are at school, an' thu grownups are working." Truman's response was a quick wag of the tail while trying to keep the cart moving.

Calvin was keeping an eye out for three straight saplings, about an inch in diameter, as they moved along. He came up with an idea that he thought might work, but he needed three staves about nine feet long. He had already collected two and just spotted the third. He whacked it down with his machete and quickly trimmed off the sucker limbs and threw it on the cart with the other two.

It was afternoon when they arrived at their first campsite. The site was only two or three miles into the swamp. Still it was hard to tell because they had used the river trails, which followed the contour of the Tensas.

Calvin was hungry, and he knew Truman was too. He had been thinking about the biscuits and leftover bacon for the past several hours.

The site was perfect. Huge cypress trees lined the banks of the river, and the dark shade of towering pin oaks prevented a lot of undergrowth. It was a natural clearing with a canopy overhead. This site had been used by "the early people" for hundreds of years. Relics and many arrowheads had been found at this very location.

He and Mr. Poole would always search for them every time they camped here. They were never lucky enough to find anything other than one small arrowhead and a few scrapers.

He unhitched Truman, and they shared the left over biscuits. They both had expended a lot of energy, and even a cold biscuit was going to hit the spot. There should be enough left for supper tonight. When that was gone, they would be on their own.

Calvin planned to keep a close eye on Truman. He was hoping he wouldn't take off back toward the store. There was every reason to think he might.

Truman took advantage of his freedom and ran around hiking a back leg to every bush he came to, marking his territory. He then scratched a little spot for a nap and lay down. Calvin, relieved he didn't bound for the road, began working on the cart.

He had noticed a two-inch ledge around the cart bed. This would allow him to bore three holes, with his skinning knife, on either side of both ledges. After sharpening the ends of the saplings, he placed one end in the hole on one side, then bent it over, creating an arch to the hole on the other side.

He emptied the cart, and without opening the tailgate, he crawled in. He was a perfect fit! With the tailgate open, there was room to lounge. Calvin collected moss and spread it evenly inside the cart, laid the quilt on top, and folded the other part over him. He had himself a warm cozy bed. *I'm uh genius! Well, that might be uh slight exaggeration*, he thought, *but it's still uh pretty good idea!*

He had been so absorbed with his project that he had taken his eyes off Truman. He was nowhere in sight. The dog had finished his nap and gotten up. Calvin was frantically searching everywhere, but he was nowhere to be seen.

"Truman, here, boy!" shouted Calvin. He repeated it as loud as he could over and over again. He realized he had just given him the name this morning, but he should've come, just hearing his voice. He was encircling the camp, ever widening as he searched, until he no longer could see the cart. Calvin whistled and even tried calling him Big'un. He was gone!

The sun was sinking lower. Shadows were getting longer, and Calvin was losing hope. Finally, hopeless, he made his way back to camp. Completely devastated, he blamed himself for not keeping him tied.

Heartbroken, he gathered kindling for a fire. He was so looking forward to his first night on the Tensas. This was not the way he had dreamed it would be.

Calvin knew he could leave everything and go back for him. But he also knew that only Truman could make the decision as to who his master would be. There was nothing Calvin could do about it.

Using kitchen matches, he started a small fire with rich heart pine from a nearby stump. He had planned to finish his canvas cover on his cart, dig a water hole in the sandbar, and get organized; but now the wind had left his sails. He didn't want to do anything. He was sick to his stomach.

Calvin watched the flames flickering from his fire and tried to pull himself back together. He just didn't know how many more highs and lows he could take. All of a sudden, he heard what sounded like a small horse, galloping through the woods.

In that moment, all was forgiven and forgotten. He leaped into the air and, with all the football skills he had acquired, tried to tackle the big beast. Again, the dog simply sidestepped him, and he went flying past, like superman without a cape.

Calvin was deliriously happy the moment he saw that wonderful dog running for him at a full gallop. He knew he was his and would be forever.

"Truman boy, let's eat." He rubbed the dog's head. "What yuh say? I'm hungry!"

After supper, which was the last of the leftovers, they sat by the fire and listened to a serenade from countless insects, frogs, and other unknown sounds of the swamp. It was their environment now, and they were not afraid; they were part of it.

Calvin spread the canvas on the ground by the fire. Truman lay down by him. He used his quilt for a pillow because now he had his dog for warmth.

CHAPTER 6

The River Bottom Home

The sun wasn't up, but they had started their day. The fire had become ashes just hours ago, and Truman was already out and about chasing rabbits or squirrels.

Calvin was cold and hungry, so the first full day of life in the bottom began by trying to correct these two problems.

He searched for firewood close by. He picked up an armload of limbs and laid them on the hot coals. It was blazing in no time, taking care of the cold problem. Now he needed to correct the hunger problem.

He let the tailgate down on his cart and used it for a surface to prepare their food. This morning, he made Johnny Cakes—fast and filling. He also cut up a couple of potatoes and added a little salt and pepper for flavor. Truman smelled the lard melting in the skillet and appeared out of nowhere. The flat cornmeal cakes and potatoes were ready in no time. They gobbled down the food and got busy with the chores.

Calvin was excited about his plans for the cart. The prospect of always having a waterproof place to sleep, on wheels, would prove to be invaluable.

He bored six holes with his skinning knife. When he had the staves in place, he draped the canvas over them and cut it to fit. After studying it for a while, he realized he could make it more efficient by trimming a couple of inches off the middle stave.

Calvin used his knife to change the angle of the front holes so the front stave would tilt forward a few inches. He did the same for the rear holes so the stave would tilt back a few inches and then tied everything in place with the heavy cord. This would keep water from running inside when it rained. *Another pretty good idea*, he thought.

Once he finished his covered wagon, he took his shovel, walked to the sandbar, and dug a two-foot deep hole. Water would seep through the sand purifying it.

Calvin went through his "to-do" list. He had water, he had shelter, and now he would need to provide food. He knew hunger pains from this point on would probably be a constant companion. He also knew this was what he had asked for. He had no regrets.

Back at the camp, Calvin took the remainder of the canvas and spread it out on the ground. He had about a five-foot square piece left. He put all his perishable goods on it and folded the sides to from a pouch. He then tied it at the top. He attached his forty-foot rope to it and threw the other end over a limb. Lifting it about twelve feet off the ground, he then tied the rope to the tree trunk. This would keep it dry and safe from hungry animals.

Calvin had other ideas to make things better for him and Truman at their campsite, but at the moment, there were more important things to do. They spent the rest of the morning checking things out up and down the river. Calvin was always aware of his surroundings; one never knows what one might find. He picked up an empty Prince Albert can, which would become his bait can for worms and grubs. It would fit perfectly in the bib pocket of his overall.

Calvin knew most of the good fishing spots within a mile or so from their camp. The water was still up and a little muddy. Pole fishing for bream probably wouldn't be that good. Instead, Calvin found a cane break and cut a dozen switch cane poles. He tied his set hooks to them and sharpened the butt end of the pole. He stuck the sharp end into the soft muddy riverbank. With these water conditions, catfish or gar would be his best bet.

The precut lines were about six feet long, with a weight tied about a foot from the catfish hook. He would bait them with whatever he could find. Calvin knew he should get his poles set right away. Catfish seem to bite better at night, but he knew as long as you had a baited hook in the water, you had a chance.

Once the cane poles were cut and lines attached, he and Truman walked the bank looking for the most productive spots. They would lay a pole and then come back later to bait the hooks and stick the poles in the soft ground. He and Truman started looking for bait. Anything would do: grubs, worms, lizards, and, of course, small fish could always be cut up and used for bait.

Calvin took the shovel for busting open logs, as well as, digging underneath them. He found enough grubs and night crawlers to bait all twelve hooks. They even found a frog. Calvin put him in his pocket, saving him for a particular spot. He remembered Mr. Poole had caught a large catfish in a deep hole underneath one of the tallest cypress trees in the bottom.

They left a pole there, but he knew a big Appaloosa would pull the pole right out of the ground. He decided to tie the line to a cypress tree limb. This required getting cold and wet. Calvin stripped naked, waded out to the cypress, and grabbed a low limb hanging over the deep hole. He pulled it around so he could tie the baited line and let it go. Once the limb swung back in place, it was in the exact spot where Mr. Poole had caught a monster catfish.

Truman was on the bank sitting on his haunches and watching the whole procedure.

Calvin's teeth chattered as he dressed. He had time to bait only one other line, when the tree limb with fresh spring foliage, began flapping on the water's surface. Suddenly, it went completely under.

Calvin ran back, still wet and cold from his first encounter with the muddy water. He stripped again but, this time, took his knife between his teeth. He waded to the cypress and cut the limb. The big Appaloosa catfish was on. Truman couldn't stand all the excitement and bailed in! Pandemonium resulted.

The scene was a boy standing on his tiptoes in nose deep water, with a sharp knife between his teeth and without a stitch on. Add to that a three-foot-long catfish, with sharp poisonous fins, wrapping the line around the boy's legs. Now throw in the mix a 140-pound canine with no earthly idea of what was going on but just wanting to be part of the action.

Truman, as one might expect, got himself caught up in the line with the catfish. Calvin, shivering and completely exhausted, managed to drag himself along with the other two onto the bank. Calvin and the catfish were lying together in a heap, covered with black mud, both gasping for breath. They looked like a couple of rare aquatic creatures, which had accidentally beached themselves. Truman was bouncing around, shaking himself dry in Calvin's face.

The fish was huge! It was the only one they caught, but it provided food for several days. The Tensas had provided.

Calvin wanted Truman to have a dry place to sleep; however, the main thing he really wanted was to keep him as close as possible. The cart was a little too low to the ground for Truman to sleep comfortably underneath, but would be perfect if it were raised a little. He used the shovel to scoop out enough dirt to allow Truman room to crawl under. He then placed palmetto palms in the enclave. *Very good!* he thought. Truman had a dry place too.

There was a light rain over night, and the morning was cold. Truman was hunkered down under the cart. Calvin marveled at how well his little shelter worked. There wasn't a drop of water inside. It was so cozy they both decided to curl up and wait out the rain.

Calvin wished he could see Truman from inside the cart, so while lying there listening to the rain, he had an idea. With his skinning knife, he bored a hole in the bottom of the cart. It took a while, but now he would be able to keep an eye on Truman. As long as he could see him, he felt much better. The peephole was finished, and without sticking his head out in the rain, he knew his dog was sleeping in. Calvin later whittled out a plug that would stop up the peephole and keep the mosquitoes out but would allow him to check on Truman.

CHAPTER 7

Moving Deeper

A few weeks had passed, and Calvin and his dog had settled into their struggle to find enough food. April, however, brings with it warmer weather and better fishing. Calvin had been searching farther and farther down the river, but since the water had receded a bit, he had been much more successful catching bluegill and catfish with a cane pole.

Calvin was determined to make their supplies last as long as possible. The potatoes were beginning to sprout, so he cut the sprouts off and ate them as a snack. If he noticed a bad spot forming on one, they would eat it first in a fish head soup with wild onions and bay leaves for seasoning.

Mr. Poole schooled the boys on plants that were eatable and those that were poison. Poke salad leaves could be eaten but only if prepared properly. As far as the Canein' Man was concerned, he had said, "If it don't kill yuh, it's eatable."

Calvin had watched Mr. Poole cook poke salad many times. They had to be young tender leaves boiled in water, drained, and boiled again. It was still a risk, so he decided not to eat poke salad unless it was a last resort. He knew the need to balance his diet with green plants. Poor health would be the one thing that would prevent him from continuing to survive in the wilderness.

His toothbrush was a black gum stem with a frayed end. He would sprinkle baking soda in his hand, dip his homemade brush in it, and brush his teeth.

Calvin wasn't the biggest fan of the washtub back at the foster home. Still, out here, it was important that he kept his body clean. Every time he got a bump or scrape, he used iodine to kill the infection. If he got hurt or sick, it would be over; he would have to go back. He knew it was the going back that he wouldn't survive.

Calvin and Truman were on the west side of the river. The land mass wasn't as wide as the east side. However, it was more remote, and the swamp followed the river for miles before reaching a road of any kind.

He and Truman were out looking for small sloughs that might have fish or bullfrogs that could be gigged, when he was surprised to see human tracks in the mud. This was the last thing he wanted to find. He knew they were still only a few miles from the bridge. It was time to move deeper into the swamp. By doing so, he hoped to avoid contact with other people. From the size of the tracks, it was two big guys, and they were walking along the riverbank.

With a sense of urgency, Calvin and Truman immediately turned around and headed back to their camp. Being spotted could present a big problem. They would have to break camp this afternoon and somehow travel at night.

The sun was sinking fast when they finally got everything packed, and Truman began pulling the cart southward. They both knew they were in for a long night. There was just enough moonlight for them to move slowly through the undergrowth without having to make a torch. Truman had much better eyesight at night than Calvin, so he let the dog take the lead.

Calvin decided to stay on higher terrain thinking the two men would probably be walking the riverbank. Truman suddenly stopped. Calvin knew he saw something and dropped to a knee, frantically trying to locate what the dog had seen.

He caught a glimpse of light flickering through the thick undergrowth. He slid an arm around Truman's neck and whispered in his ear, "Stay, boy." They froze in one spot, not moving a muscle for what seemed like an eternity. They could hear two men talking. It wasn't clear what the conversation was about; but from the tone, flavor, and use of profanity, he could tell they weren't reciting their Sunday school lesson.

Calvin could hear the hollow muffled sound of things being loaded into a wooden boat and paddles banging on the sides. He was relieved. This meant they were staying on the other side of the river. There were a few people who lived on the eastside; some were homesteaders and for the most part were good folks, but there were some really bad river rats also. They were moonshiners and had bad reputations with the law.

They watched and listened as the light and chatter faded into the opposite bank. Calvin knew he would need to stay clear of these two and hoped they hadn't seen their camp. From this point on, they would be more careful.

Once assured all was clear, they continued their slow progress. Calvin was using his machete to keep the mud from building up on the wheels. He cut a sapling here and there from the path. This was new territory for Calvin, but the Canein' Man had told him about a small lake with lots of bluegill, frogs, and crawfish that could be obtained many different ways. If he were to camp between the lake and river, the potential for fishing different types of water would make chances of success better. This information provided them with a destination, but having never been there, he had little hope of actually finding it. After all, the Tensas River Bottom covers about eighty thousand acres.

They traveled all the next day until the sun was almost down and they were too tired to go any farther. Calvin unhitched the dog, took the small canvas, and spread it out on the ground, leaving everything else inside the cart. He boiled the last of the potatoes and, with what little energy he had left, made Johnny Cakes. They were bone-tired.

After eating, they stretched out on the canvas pallet and slept until early morning.

It was nearly daylight when Truman sprang from the canvas and went running wildly through the woods. Calvin jumped up and ran after him. The chase was on! A large swamp rabbit ran for cover and crawled into a hollow tree.

The swamp hare climbed up into the hollow tree too far for them to reach him. They were left with a couple of options: build a fire, put damp leaves on it, and smoke him out or cut a long flexible stick with a forked end, run the stick up the hollow tree until they reached the varmint, then twist it into his fur and pull him out. They went with the first option.

When smoke began to boil out from every opening of the old snag, the varmint could stand it no longer. He tried to escape the way he went in, but Truman heard him turn inside the hollow and was ready. As soon as he came out, the big dog immediately grabbed him.

Calvin cleaned the rabbit with his skinning knife and pitched the skin, with the head still attached to Truman. He caught it in his mouth and inhaled it with one gulp. They both were excited. Calvin shouted out loud, "I got me uh huntin' dog too. Yuh can do everything, can't yuh, boy!"

They both danced around, celebrating their success. It wasn't long before they had him roasting on the fire. The roasted rabbit was by far the best meal he and Truman had eaten since they entered the swamp. After all the meat was cleaned off the bones, he gave them to Truman, and once again they were gone in a blink of an eye.

"That was quite tasty. We got 'a do that again," said Calvin. He loved fish, but the thought of a little red meat, from time to time, would make things much better. The rabbit was more than a good meal; it was a symbol of the possibilities of what he and his dog were capable of when they worked together.

Calvin had been shaping a bow over the past few weeks. His arrows would be made from any hard straight sticks he could find, which would allow him to attach feathers to the small end and sharpen the other end.

Calvin had already made a spear that could be used for multiple purposes. If they were able to find the oxbow lake the Canein' Man had told him about, he could wade the shallow edges at night with his bow and take alligator gar and bullfrogs—and, after a lot of practice, perhaps even ducks.

From the Canein' Man's directions, the lake should be within reach before the sun went down.

An oxbow lake is formed over hundreds of years when a river slowly changes course and a small portion of the original river becomes isolated. They are very common and add a different type of water to the environment. It's more placid water than river water and would attract different types of birds and animals than the river. It would have large numbers of crawfish. Calvin loved crawfish, so he was hoping they could find it.

Once the wheels were cleaned, they were off again. Calvin could see a small slough ahead. It was not more than a couple of feet deep at any point. He knew this wasn't the lake but would be worth checking out. Calvin spotted something unusual sticking out of the water.

"Hey, Truman, what do yuh think that is, buddy boy?" As they got closer, he realized it was some type of net.

Someone had seined this little body of water for fish bait and had left the seine.

"Wow, look at what we found!" he shouted. "We'll catch us some crawfish. Yuh do like crawfish, don't yuh, boy? We'll boil 'em up with salt an' pepper, an' I bet we can find some wild onions too! Ah, come on, buddy boy, yuh gone 'a love 'em." Truman was not responding.

It was a cloudy overcast day, but he could tell the sun was vertical. They decided to take a break and retrieve the net. Calvin took his shoes off, rolled up the cuffs on his overalls, waded over, and picked up the end of the seine, which was in the water.

The net was about twelve feet long, with poles on both ends. It appeared that someone stuck one pole in the mud, stretched the net out, and dragged it in a circle close to the bottom, hoping to catch something. Obviously, there was no one to hold the other end, and since Truman didn't have opposable thumbs, he would try the same tactic.

Calvin pushed his end of the seine at an angle along the bottom of the slough, hoping to trap something in the net. He made a complete circle, quickly lifted his end, twisted the net to trap whatever was inside, pulled the other end up, and dragged it to the bank.

Truman ran over to help him check out the catch. Calvin pulled the net to dry ground and untwisted it to expose their catch. There were several silver bait-size fish, three small bream, all flipping and flouncing the length of the net. For Calvin, the best part of the catch was several dozen crawfish, which were trying to back all the way to the water. Truman bent down to nose a crawfish but quickly jumped back wearing a couple from his upper lip.

Calvin laughed. "Watch out, big boy. They're gone 'a eat yuh alive."

He grabbed his tub, scooped a little water in it, then dropped in the catch and tied the tub to the side of the cart. He was ecstatic, knowing his new acquisition could be the difference between survival and starvation. He rolled up the net, placed it inside the cart, hitched the big dog, and proceeded in search of the mythical lake.

Having had roasted rabbit, they collected everything else that was edible, along their path. They looked for openings that were less than 50 percent shade. Calvin searched for wild plums, different grasses, ferns, flowers, dew berries, black berries, water crest, cattails, and dandelions. The vegetation provided the balanced diet he needed.

Truman was a true carnivore but actually nibbled on some grass occasionally. This helped with digestion. They both liked the dewberries that grew close to the ground. No matter if they were ripe or green, they were tasty and plentiful this time of year.

Chapter 8

The Oxbow

The sun was dropping low in the sky. Calvin had no way of knowing for sure but thought they had traveled about ten miles since they left the road. He kept his eyes on the ground looking for human tracks but, thankfully, hadn't seen any.

"Hey, look uh there, Truman! There it is! We found it! It's thu oxbow!" Calvin shouted. "That has ta be it! Ain't it beautiful, Truman?"

All it took for Calvin to snap out of his troubling thoughts was a glimpse of shimmering water through the dark silhouettes of the tall trees.

He quickly surveyed for camping sites. He knew it would be best to stay on the eastside of the lake in order to have easy access to both the river and lake. The Canein' Man was right again; what a great place to set up camp! Calvin found a spot that had a little elevation. Water would run off in case of rain, and it would also give him good visibility in all directions. He quickly unhitched Truman and began to set up.

Calvin was hoping he could find a spring with good water so he wouldn't have to carry water from a sandbar near the creek. The Canein' Man told him there were springs in this area. He still had enough drinking water in his canvas bag for a couple of days. He would look for a spring tomorrow. He could always boil the water when he needed. But now he was excited about setting up the camp.

Truman was enjoying a moment of freedom. He set off lifting a hind leg to every bush in his path to mark his new territory. Calvin wanted to stay here as long as possible. It was deep enough in the swamp that chance encounters with people would be slim.

The campsite would provide maximum hunting and fishing. There were cane breaks for fishing poles, as well as openings around the shallow end of the lake, which would attract waterfowl. The site would provide many eatable plants, such as dandelions, watercress, berries, and cattails. The palmettos, in some places, were seven feet tall! These would be used to make a lean-to. The palmetto berries, as for as Calvin was concerned, were eatable but only as a last resort. There were several wild pecan trees that would have nuts in the fall.

Calvin knew squirrels like to eat the fresh buds on most hard woods. The Canein' Man had informed Calvin that Truman was a squirrel dog. He would chase the squirrel up a tree and then alert Calvin by barking. Once he was good enough to hit one with his bow, there would always be a chance for red meat, as well as, fish.

This will be home for a long time, thought Calvin. He would make the best camp possible. The first thing he needed, however, was a campfire. He would cook Truman some hot water bread and fry a small mess of fish, along with crawfish tails for himself.

Calvin cleaned both the fish and crawfish, saving the heads for Truman's bread. He put a little water in his pot and placed it on the fire. When it started boiling, he added cornmeal and stirred in the heads for protein. After melting lard in the frying pan, he dropped in scoops of the cornmeal and fried it. When Truman's bread was made, he mealed some of the small fish and crawfish tails, added a little salt and pepper, then fried them in the hot grease for himself.

They ate their fill. Calvin almost felt guilty eating something that tasted so good. Out here, it was about survival. They would only eat to survive, but what the heck—he thought—if it tasted good what harm would that do!

It didn't look like rain and the nights were warming up. Calvin decided he would leave everything inside his cart and sleep by the fire on the small canvas. He hoped, at some point, his pal Truman would curl up beside him.

Now it's all about food. Next day, they were in the cane patch gathering poles for fishing and a lean-to. He emptied the cart, hitched Truman, and loaded them. The cart held at least fifty or so and would be more than enough for both needs.

He took twelve polls, tied lines on them, and headed for the river. He had found grubs and night crawlers, enough to bait the hooks. Again, he knew if he had baited hooks in the water, he had a chance.

They went back to camp to search for water. Hopefully, they would find a natural spring that wouldn't require boiling the water.

Calvin grabbed his gig and tow sack—might as well try to find a bullfrog or two while they were looking. If he was lucky enough to find water close by, this would be a perfect place to stay.

His thoughts wandered to "the early people" living here thousands of years ago. What a privilege for him, and the best dog anyone could have, to share the same experience!

One of his favorite memories of Mr. Poole was the two of them fishing the Tensas. While fishing, Mr. Poole would quote from Henry David Thoreau's *Walden Pond*. It was on such occasions Calvin began longing for the freedom of living off the land as his ancestors had. He knew in his heart this experience wouldn't last forever; nothing ever did. But they were here now and would live in the moment.

They had no frogs in their sack. On the way back, he spotted Truman lapping water. From a distance, it appeared to be just a hole in the ground. On closer observation, he realized water was bubbling from a tiny spring not more than thirty yards from the camp. He knelt down beside Truman, put one arm around his neck, and said, "Yuh can do it all, can't yuh, boy . . . even find water!" With the other hand, Calvin scooped up a cupped handful of cold clear water.

Over the next few days, Calvin built the lean-to. He cut two polls with a fork at the top and put them a couple of feet in the ground, about ten feet apart. Standing on his tub, he then laid a long pole across the top forks and tied it down with pieces of cord. He placed the bamboo canes about a foot apart against the top pole forming the lean-to. He finished it by cutting and laying palmetto palms on top in layers thick enough to make it waterproof. There was room enough for himself, Truman, and the cart.

He took six or eight cane polls. Tying the top ends together, he stood them up and spread the bottom ends out, forming a teepee. Calvin covered the teepee with palmetto palms, making a fish smoker. He would check the set poles every morning. Any fish not consumed the day it was caught would be salted and smoked.

He spread palmetto palms underneath the lean-to shelter to serve as a floor. Every day, he would add something to make it a little better and more comfortable.

The swamp was providing a living between the oxbow, the Tensas River, and whatever game they could hunt and trap. Though it was a constant struggle, he was now a hunter-gatherer, like most primitive people before him. He and Truman would survive on what they could provide for themselves.

Calvin made loop snares out of baling wire he had found. These were placed in trails used by rabbits and other game and checked daily. He built stick traps that could be used for birds and squirrels. He would lay pieces of cane in a square, tying the ends together, each smaller than the other creating a pyramid shape. Once the trap was baited, he would lift one side with a hair trigger. It would fall with the slightest touch.

Of course, his set poles were always baited and in the water. He also made fish traps using cane wrapped with muscadine and other wild grapevines. The traps were weighed down with rocks tied to a tree limb and then placed on the river bottom. They were baited with fish and animal parts, hoping to catch bottom feeders, such as catfish, buffalo, gasper goo, and maybe even a few crawfish.

Calvin cut a three-foot piece off one end of his seine to make a dip net, which had a bamboo handle. He wrapped a long flexible twig around his small tub and let it dry. This formed the hoop to tie the net to. It was handy for catching minnows. He used the tiny fish for crappie, bass, and anything that preferred live bait.

His work was never done. When he finished the task at hand, his thoughts would turn to what needed to be done next. Truman did his part to contribute. His excursions usually produced a freshly caught rabbit, which Calvin would cook, and they would share.

They became opportunists. The boy and his dog took advantage of what the swamp offered. Calvin would hang his bow over his shoulder and grab a handful of arrows, and the hunting party would leave camp before daylight. His skills with his bow improved because of necessity. Birds, bullfrogs, fish, and most anything that presented itself were now in mortal danger.

The pair learned to hunt in unison, instinctively knowing what the other needed done. If they spotted a squirrel in a tree, Calvin would remain still as Truman would circle to the other side, grab a bush in his mouth, and shake it so the varmint would slide to the opposite side, giving Calvin a better shot.

Like all primitive hunters before them, they were respectful of the game they took. They used every part of the animal they killed either as food or bait. Even as proficient as they had become, they were usually hungry and constantly looking for the next meal.

The days were warming. Calvin took the opportunity to go barefooted because his shoes were becoming too tight. It wasn't long before the bottoms of his feet were becoming like leather. He was out doors all the time, so his tan was getting darker, and his mop of hair grew lighter and longer each day. The one thing he forgot was a pair of scissors. His appearance was changing; he looked more like a resident of the swamp. Though this wasn't his favorite, several times a week he took a rag and a bar of lava soap down to the river and washed from head to toe.

Unfortunately, the advent of warming weather brought with it several unwanted guests: mosquitoes and reptiles. The swamp was full of snakes, some harmless and some not.

The cottonmouth was the most numerous and the one Calvin feared the most. They lived where both he and the dog would most likely be found hunting and fishing. They were perfectly camouflaged and deadly.

Rattlesnakes were hidden in the canebrakes; at least they would give a warning before a strike. Not so with the cottonmouth. They arrived in this world with a nasty disposition and an even worse attitude. Calvin was repulsed by the puffy white mouth gaping from the coils of its short muscular body. He was constantly on guard for them but noticed Truman seemed to be oblivious. He would plow through the most foreboding-looking marsh with little regard to what might be lurking within.

A few days after pitching camp, Calvin was fishing with a cane pole from a low flat bank. He had caught several nice bluegills, strung them on his homemade ten-foot-long stringer, and stuck the wooden tip in the ground next to him.

Truman was tiptoeing in the water along the edge of the bank, pawing at who-knows-what and totally messing the fishing up. The warm sun was causing Calvin to nod, so he leaned back against a tree trunk, slipping in and out of sleep.

Suddenly, the splashing of water jerked him back into consciousness. Truman had managed to wrap the stringer around one of his back legs, causing him to panic because it wouldn't come off. Truman bolted for the bank with it still attached. Calvin couldn't believe his eyes. There was a huge ball of writhing, shimmering, serpents coiled around the handful of perch, which were being consumed while still attached to the stringer.

Truman turned to see what was hot on his trail and looking for help, ran straight for Calvin. Calvin realized the gravity of the situation and leaped to his feet. Because of the load Truman was pulling, he was able to run neck and neck with the big dog. With a megashot of adrenaline, pulsating through their veins, they both ran frantically through the woods with little regard for the others' well-being. In other words, it was every man for himself. They managed to distribute a line of irritated cottonmouth snakes fifty yards long throughout the swamp.

The camp was working well. There was plenty of room in the lean-to for both to sleep inside. Most nights, there was no need to sleep close to the fire, so Calvin made it farther from their shelter. The fire would still provide a sense of well-being and keep animals away from their camp. He didn't have candles or an oil lamp for a night-light.

Calvin knew how to render oil from animal fat, but it would require more time and effort than he could justify. He made a few torches by tying bundles of dry straw together. He kept them close to his bed because there were a couple of times over the last week or two he awoke and Truman wasn't there. He felt much safer with him close by.

He was curious why Truman felt the need to leave him and sometimes wander off during the night. The fact he had always come back was by far the most important thing; however, he still was a little offended. There seemed to be a primeval side of him that he couldn't understand. Possibly, because his ancestors, like all dogs, were once wolves. It was obvious the dog could hear things that Calvin wasn't capable of hearing.

Truman would become uneasy and get up and stare into the blackness with a sense of yearning. Sometimes he would return to his bed, but other times he would leave and wouldn't return until the next day. Calvin was so afraid something would happen and he wouldn't or couldn't return.

The fish smoker was a draw for wild animals, and without Truman's protection, he would be in a great deal of danger if he continued using it.

There were still a lot of black bear in the Tensas River Bottom, along with coyotes, wolves, and panthers. Things always seemed to be the scariest and the most troublesome during the wee hours of morning. The danger from predator animals was real, but then there were the mythical creatures. They seemed even scarier, especially at night.

Calvin, as all kids in this neck of the woods, had heard stories of a monster living in the swamps of Louisiana. It was described as a big hairy apelike creature that looked as if it was covered with moss. He wasn't sure that anything like that really existed; however, he had to admit, lying there, his mind conjured up images that were disturbing for a kid.

The sun was going down, and the inevitable night song was starting up, when Calvin was suddenly jarred to the bone. It happened every time he heard the mournful call of a whip-poor-will. The sound caused all the other occupants of the swamp to fall silent, for a moment, even though it was a common sound for a warm spring night in the river bottom.

Calvin's reaction to a whip-poor-will's call was different from most people because it always reminded him of a story that Mr. Poole once told the boys on a camping trip.

Mr. Poole said the whip-poor-will is perhaps the most timid and elusive of all the birds in the swamp. Very few people have ever seen one in their natural habitat. Its camouflage is without equal. Their feathers look like the scaly bark of a dead tree. The whip-poor-will becomes invisible before one's eyes as it sits on a limb. They are very shy and almost never seen in daylight.

The story Mr. Poole shared with the boys was so bizarre. Calvin would instantly think of it every time he heard the cry of a whip-poor-will.

When he was a young boy, Mr. Poole's family had a neighbor who became a widow shortly after the birth of her youngest son, Will. The boy was born with deformed legs and never able to walk. He pulled himself around on the floor with his arms, developing a superstrong upper body, but had tiny useless legs. He would occasionally hug his mother so tightly with those massive arms it was frightening. She would have to pry them apart to get her breath.

He was the youngest of several kids. The others grew older and moved away. Finally, it was just him and his beloved mother. She loved and adored her son, who totally depended on her.

As the years passed, her health began to fail, and it became difficult for her to care for the boy. Though Will was almost grown, he still possessed the mind of a child. Even though it was difficult to care for him all by herself, she refused any help from the neighbors or relatives.

One day, she notified the community that her seventeen-year-old son, Will, had passed away. She would hold a wake for him at her home near the edge of the woods. Folks began arriving that afternoon, bringing food and preparing to sit up through the night with her and the deceased.

Walker Poole was just a young boy but went along with his mother and two older sisters. He had never attended a wake and was very nervous about it.

Upon arrival, they were greeted by the boy's mother and escorted to the bedroom, where she had laid the corpse out on his bed. There was hushed mumbling from the gathering, which was made up of mostly women. Walker was shocked at how peaceful the boy looked, just as though he were only taking a nap.

The warm spring evening and the crowded room required the window to be open, allowing the white lace curtains to gently move with the breeze.

This was the first dead person Walker had ever seen. He was overwhelmed with sadness for the boy and his mother; however, she seemed quite peaceful. She was busy taking food and placing it on the kitchen table. People were crammed in the small bedroom, and it was standing room only.

The soft rays from the evening sun streamed through the open window, illuminating the room and the blond hair neatly arranged on the boy's head. What happened next defies all explanation.

Will's mother stood at the foot of the bed and asked if everyone would join her in singing a few courses of "Amazing Grace" for *Poor Will*. At that moment, a whippoor-will, the most reclusive of all birds, flew in the open window of the crowded room and perched on the bedpost next to the boy's body.

***

Calvin didn't sleep well. He had a very unpleasant dream and woke itching like crazy. The mosquitoes almost carried him off during the night. He knew smoke would help with the mosquito problem, but that required too much effort to keep the fire going just right to create smoke. He might have to start sleeping in the cart again with the flaps closed. There are some plants that could be used for repellent: lemon grass, soybean, wild garlic, and lavender; but he had none of these at the moment.

Since the arrival of hordes of mosquitoes, Calvin's biggest fear was squatting behind a bush for his morning routine. He made sure he had a good handful of perfect leaves in order to finish the job in a hurry.

Calvin was also a little anxious this morning because Truman wasn't there. He called him a few times and then, from the back side of the lake, heard him running for the camp. Just knowing Truman was still there was always such a relief.

Truman greeted Calvin for a pat on the head. He now considered Calvin his master, and that was his way of acknowledging it. Calvin knew Truman belonged to him, but it was still hard to believe. How could a five-foot nothing of a boy be worthy of having this Goliath of a dog?

Chapter 9

Wild Boar Fight

Even though Calvin had experienced a lot more hardships than most his age, being a young boy has its advantages. He was thrilled at the prospect of adventure promised with each new day in the swamp. The main obstacle, as always, was how to fill their empty bellies. The quest that never ended.

The provisions he got from the store were almost gone. Over the next few weeks, he would learn to depend on the river and marsh for survival.

Calvin never cared for candy that much. He enjoyed an ice cream cone, on occasion, from the Smith Grocery; but fruit and berries of all kinds were his favorites. The one thing he did miss most was watermelon.

Mr. Poole always had a garden and tried to raise watermelons, but the black delta soil was not very good for that particular crop. The sandy soil of North Louisiana was the best.

Mr. Poole had a good friend, Lawrence Wells, who lived over in Jonesboro. He raised the best watermelons in the country and always brought the foster home a truckload. He was just that kind of guy.

Every year about this time, Calvin would begin to crave the cool, sweet, juicy red meat of Mr. Wells' watermelons.

The boy and his dog were out early resetting the cane poles, hoping for better results. They still had a dozen or so smoked gar, but Calvin wanted some fresh bluegill.

After baiting the set hooks, he took a pole and made his way farther down the river than he had ever ventured before, stopping to search for bait along the way. He would take his skinning knife and dig in the soft ground for earthworms and grubs to fill his old Prince Albert tobacco can. He rigged his pole with a line almost as long as the twelve-foot pole, then added a cork and a small lead weight with a small bream hook.

Calvin found a deep hole of water with a large cypress in the middle of it. He was on the cutting side of the river. Over time, the current had undercut the soft river sand, creating a steep bank. There was a log lying on the bank, and the small end cantilevered eight feet or so over the water. He decided to straddle the log and scoot out to the end. This would allow him to fish next to the cypress. He knew big bluegill loved to hang around the folds of the cypress.

It wasn't long before the cork moved slightly, went completely under, and disappeared into the dark murky water of the Tensas. Calvin lifted the pole and felt the weight of a big fat bluegill bream. With much skill and experience, he allowed the big perch to make circles in the water. Each circle led him ever closer to the surface. Then as soon as he broke free of the water's gravity, he lifted the pole straight up with his right hand and, with barely a ripple, swung the brightly colored perch to his left hand. He grabbed the line just above the fish. Then took his stringer and strung him up. This was by far the most enjoyable way of providing protein for him and Truman.

He pulled one big bluegill after the other from the shady side of the cypress tree. All the flouncing around on the water surface attracted some gar fish, and they began to strike the bait before it had a chance to sink.

Calvin decided to see if he could jerk a couple of smaller ones out. He wrapped the line around the end of his pole until it was only about three feet long, took the cork off, and added a catfish hook.

The idea was to dangle the bait on the water surface in order to entice a strike. Gars have a long snout with rows of sharp teeth, so the best approach was to jerk it quickly over his head to the bank behind. He was successful, and six gar about two or three feet long were flopping around on the ground behind him. Smoked or boiled, one of these big guys each day was enough for Truman. Anything else he could find was a bonus.

Calvin hadn't seen him in awhile and was about to give him a whistle, when he heard some grunting and squealing. He quickly glanced around and saw a terrifying sight. There were several little bluish gray-striped pigs and the mother sow, eating one of the gar. Calvin knew there was nothing more vicious than a sow with baby pigs. Calvin immediately realized he was in trouble. He was perched on the end of the log with no way off, except to jump in the river.

The only thing he could do was hope he wouldn't be seen. He decided just to sit it out and wait until they had finished. Maybe she would never know he was there. But, as luck would have it, he spotted two large boars with sharp tusk protruding from their long snouts, in a full run to join the feast. The dinner on the ground attracted another dozen squealing, grunting, quarreling wild hogs. They had now surrounded Calvin's log, trying to get their share of the fish. They were only a few feet away but still unaware of his presence. He was barely breathing.

There were only two options: sit motionless until they left or jump in the river. The river was too swift and wide for him to swim to the other side. If he jumped in the river, he would still have to climb up the bank on this side where they would surely be waiting for him.

Calvin sat straddling the log for what seemed like an hour. Mosquitoes were biting, and his legs began to cramp. He could stand it no longer and was going to have to move! He decided to swing around on the log and scream as loud as he could at the same time. Maybe this would scare them off.

His scream caused a small stampede. The hogs scampered in all directions. Three of them, the mother sow and the two big boars, froze in position. Small black beady eyes glared at Calvin.

All at once, both boars rushed to the base of the log, flashing and snapping their tusks. They had become irritated when the little pigs squealed and ran. Black mane was raised on their backs. One was actually trying to climb onto the log.

Calvin broke off the tip of his pole and used the butt end to jab at the wild beast. The animal was so enraged that he cut his own tongue with his slashing tusk. Blood and saliva were spewing from his grotesque mouth. He was hell-bent on getting to Calvin and managed to get too close for comfort. If he actually walked the log, the only choice Calvin had was not whether to jump but where to jump.

Just as he was about to leap, there was a loud flurry of growling and squealing. Truman had latched onto the wild boar's back leg. Being drug backward, the irate swine spun around and drove slashing tusk toward his tormentor's rib cage. Truman released his grip and jumped aside as the hog lounged forward like a bull charging the matador's cape.

Then, as quick as a leopard, Truman leaped for the throat, pinning him to the ground. The sounds of the death struggle, emitting from the two combatants, caused the other big boar to join the fight. Using his long snout armed with protruding tusk, he began to slash at Truman's back legs but the dog wouldn't let go and continued to squeeze life from his adversary.

Calvin didn't hesitate; he flung himself into the battle. He was beating the hog's nose with the butt end of the cane pole, hoping to prevent him from cutting Truman's legs. Calvin could see blood running down both. He became enraged and began jabbing with the sharp end of the pole at the animal's eyes.

When this didn't stop him, Calvin lost all fear for his own well-being and took his skinning knife, leaped astride the beast, and drove it deep into his neck. The hog let out a loud squeal and spun around, throwing Calvin to the ground. With blood gushing from his neck, he ran about trying to escape the pain, blindly crashing into everything in his path.

Calvin jumped up, grabbed Truman around the neck, and finally pulled him from the lifeless wild hog. He frantically rubbed all over his entire body, especially his rib cage, looking to see if there was any life-threatening wounds. He and Truman were both covered with blood from head to toe, so he couldn't tell for sure how badly he was hurt. Calvin was relieved. He didn't think Truman would die from any of the wounds, but the loss of blood was taking its toll.

The wounds on his back legs were gushing blood, and he was beginning to tremble. Calvin was afraid he would go into shock. He made Truman lie down so he could examined the wounds more closely. There was one that looked especially bad. He took his knife belt and strapped it around the dog's leg above the deep gash, then applied pressure to the wound. He watched as the blood slowly began to coagulate. Still he was extremely worried.

Truman had lost a lot of blood and was too weak to walk. Calvin knew he would have to find a way to get him back to camp. He cut two long straight poles and used some of the cord from the fish stringer to tie the small ends together. While it was on the ground, he spread the bottom ends about three feet apart, then laid smaller limbs across them and tied them in place. He laid a few palmetto palms across for a bed.

Truman weighed a 140 pounds, but Calvin knew he had to get him to camp. He managed to get Truman onto the slide, stepped inside, and began the difficult journey back to camp. It was almost dark when they arrived. Calvin wasn't sure what he needed to do, but he was determined to save his dog's life.

First, he cleaned the wounds with water, then took the iodine along with some of the Vaseline and made a paste. Calvin applied it to all the wounds, except the really bad one. This one would require some stitches. He used his knife blade to circle around the tip of a sharp palmetto palm about an inch down from the tip. He bent the tip back and forth until it broke loose and pulled the fibers out, creating a needle with thread. There was some moonlight, but he needed more light. Calvin made a fire, lit two of the torches for more light, and prepared to stitch the four-inch cut.

Never having done anything like this before, he wasn't sure Truman would just lie there and allow him to stick a sharp object in his back leg. The big dog barely flinched. It required several tips from palmetto palms, but it actually worked, and the wound was finally closed. After taking the tourniquet off, he applied the salve. He then gave Truman a drink of water and tied a strip of cloth around the wound.

Lying by the fire, Calvin relived the whole incident in his mind. He was humbled by the way Truman had come to his defense, and he had to smile to himself at what he had done. Unfortunately, there was no one to witness the amazing event.

Before he ever left for the swamp, he had promised himself that he would no longer think like a young white boy, and he didn't.

"By golly, I can't believe I actually did that! I guess I was too scared, ta be scared," he admitted to himself.

Calvin was delighted to see how Truman was recovering. He was literally licking his wounds and wasn't too fond of the ointment Calvin had applied. Now that he had licked most of it off, he was licking his paws, trying to get it off his tongue.

Calvin began to think of the two hundred pounds or more of protein the big wild boar would provide after it was dressed and cut up. He could use the slide, and the moonlight would give him enough light to make his way back to the kill site. The problem would be how to make sure Truman didn't try to come with him. He stood up, got his hatchet, and tied it to the slide. Stepping inside, he kept one eye on Truman.

"Stay, boy," he said with a stern voice, although he knew Truman would do what he wanted and there was nothing he could do about it.

The distance back through the woods was about a mile, but it would take some time navigating only by moonlight and a torch. He began inching along, not sure he would be able to find the trail or be able stay on it if he found it.

The swamp had its usual eerie look and feel in the moonlight. Spanish moss draped over everything, making it look like the setting for a scary movie. He had only seen one, a *Dracula* picture show, which he hadn't completely recovered from.

Otis and Mattie Smith, owners of the store, had a second business—a mobile picture show. The movie was projected from the back of his old canvas-topped military truck onto a screen inside a tent. The Pooles took all the foster kids to see the picture show, thinking it was a Western movie but, as it turned out, was *Dracula the Vampire*. Calvin was more scared of the make-believe character he had seen on the screen than the real blood-and-bone wild boar he had jumped and straddled. Sometimes, the imaginary is more frightening than reality. With the scary image of the hunched-over pale-faced boney-fingered monster Count Dracula, he kept slowly making his way through the swamp.

Everything was now cast in a bluish tint from the moonlight, causing the swamp to have a faded look. Then from his peripheral view, a dark shape moved in the distance.

"What was that?" he said to himself. Calvin stopped, frantically trying to see it again. He stood frozen in mid-step, but nothing moved, and the dark shape wasn't there anymore. Maybe his mind was playing tricks on him; maybe it was Dracula with his black cape. That image was tattooed on his brain from the movie he had seen as a six-year-old. Could it be the swamp monster? Whatever it was, it was now gone. He was ashamed at how quickly he reverted back to the eleven-year-old when Truman wasn't by his side.

He slowly moved forward again, with his head now on a swivel, looking all directions at once. The plan was to gut the hog, cut it in pieces, and then pull it back to camp on the slide. He was well aware of the work involved. He had helped Mr. Poole slaughter domestic hogs many times in the past. The difference being they would dip the whole farm-raised pig in scalding water to loosen the hair and then scrap it off. There was no way he physically could do that. Once he packed it back to camp, he would remove the hair one ham at a time.

Calvin tried to stay within hearing distance of the river. Once he felt he had gone a mile, he should be close to the clearing where the boar would be. Either the moon was getting brighter, or his eyes had grown accustomed to the dark, because he was able to see better now, than when he started.

He couldn't believe it; he actually spotted the dark silhouette of the hog lying on the ground and what looked like a couple of dogs tearing at his soft underbelly. It was coyotes, but he knew once they saw him they would run. They weren't a threat to him, but he also knew coyotes weren't what he had seen earlier. They caught a glimpse of the boy, reluctantly pulled themselves away from a potential meal, and disappeared into the swamp.

The coyotes had torn a hole in his belly, and he had already bled out. This was a good thing because the weather was a little too warm for hog butchering. The sooner the blood was removed, the better the meat would be.

He took his large skinning knife and cut him open, from one end to the other, and removed the entrails, saving the heart, liver, and kidneys. Calvin used his hatchet to cut through bone, separating the hams, shoulders, and ribs.

He wasn't sure how he had gotten Truman back to camp, but he had heard under extreme stress one may possess superhuman strength. That had to explain it; but now, looking at the pile of meat, there was no way he could carry more than fifty pounds at a time.

The torch was more trouble than it was worth. Now with only moonlight to see by, he decided to make several trips. The first would consist of both shoulders and organs. It was now almost midnight. By the time he made the last trip back and hung it all in his smoker, it would probably be morning.

Calvin was beginning to buckle under the strain; this was by far the most stressful day since leaving home. He was hungry, thirsty, and tired; but he knew this was a rare opportunity, and he was determined to finish the job. He kept his head down and focused on the task at hand.

There are a lot of scary things in the swamp, some real, others imaginary; but he had to get the meat to the camp. He strained against the load, stopping to rest every hundred yards. With only about fifty yards left, he stopped one last time, with the glow of the campfire in sight.

He saw the big dog stand up and start hobbling toward him. Calvin's heart leapt, for he knew he was going to be okay. It wasn't possible for Calvin to love Truman any more than he did at this moment. He stepped out of the slide and met him halfway. Calvin walked him back to the camp and made him lay back down.

Calvin sliced up some of the liver and fried it in the skillet. They both needed protein, and the iron rich organ was perfect. Truman displayed a hearty appetite and responded immediately. It was a miraculous recovery for them both.

Truman walked a little stiff legged but made the next two trips with Calvin. They retrieved all of the meat, including the head. After working through the night, they both needed rest. It was almost noon before Calvin started the smoking process.

He cut green oak for smoking the meat. Calvin had to enlarge the smoker to accommodate the big hog. He dipped the hams and shoulders one at a time in his tub of boiling water to loosen the stiff black hair before scraping them. What hair was left, he lit a torch and singed it off. The hams were rubbed with salt and hung inside the smoker. The ribs were skinned; he planned to eat them before they spoiled.

Calvin knew if he was able to keep the blowflies off, smoke and dry the meat, they would have food for weeks. After the meat was hung, he planned to stay close to camp and ward off hungry animals that couldn't resist the aroma of smoked pork. This would give Truman time to completely recover. Now Calvin had time to do some things at the camp that he, otherwise, wouldn't be able to do.

Calvin boiled the head. Not only was there a lot of protein to be found, he wanted to cut out the tusk. Over the next few days, he drilled a hole in one of the tusk with his knife and wore it around his neck as a badge of courage. In his mind, he was becoming more and more Indian.

CHAPTER 10

The Encounter

Calvin didn't feel he had used the traps to their full potential. This would be a great opportunity to keep them set, check them on a regular basis, and still be able to stay close to camp. He also would have some time to practice his bow skill by hunting for birds and frogs around the oxbow lake.

Calvin's spear was nothing more than a sharpened stick made from the sapling he cut beneath the bridge. He had been thinking of a way to make his spear a more durable and lethal weapon. With this extra time available, he would upgrade his spear.

Taking his file, he placed it across two rocks, and with a sharp blow from the blunt side of his hatchet, it broke into. This left two-thirds for a file and a tip for the point of his spear. He attached the sharp point to the peeled sapling, making a far superior spear than just a sharpened stick.

He set snares along trails and placed fish traps in the lake. With a supply of protein, he was able to gather berries, wild onions, and some fresh young tender leafy plants. He grazed like an animal. He also pulled young green cattails from the lake and cut the tender bottom section into strips. They would provide much-needed roughage. He had to admit that there were several things he had to force himself to eat. Cattails, by themselves, was one. Muscles, along the riverbank, was the other. He didn't care for either, but they made good soup with pork bones.

Calvin loved venison. He had never killed a deer, because it was Mr. Poole's responsibility to provide it for the foster home. Calvin decided not to try to hunt for deer. He could possibly hit one with his bow and arrow, but without a metal point or stone, he wouldn't be able to bring him down. Unless there were some unusual circumstances, he didn't plan on eating deer meat in the swamp.

Calvin made arrows from small straight saplings. He would cut them the right length and peel the bark off. Then he would create a sharp end by scraping it with his knife while turning it over the fire. He would save large feathers for the small end, then cut and attach them with boiled sweet gum and pine rosin glue, like his ancestors did. He would have to keep sharpening the tip after each hunt.

He had gathered an extra-large pile of Spanish moss, which he used some for bedding. Then he mixed some of it with mud into the shape of a wild hog. This he used as a target and practiced every opportunity he had. Over time, he became a good shot and a deadly hunter.

Calvin was grateful for each animal he killed with the bow. He took no delight in the taking of a life, large or small. He took only what he and Truman needed to survive.

The meat was cured after about a month of drying and smoking. Calvin took it from the smoker and laid the meat on the small piece of canvas, pulled it up on all sides, and tied the top with a piece of cord. He used the long plow-line to hoist it about ten feet off the ground. This would keep animals from getting it, but the aroma was picked up by the breeze and carried throughout the swamp. The camp smelled like a backyard barbecue joint. That made Calvin nervous; he knew there were bears and other animals already casing the place.

Calvin was up before the sun. He slipped out of his long handles and stepped into his overalls. With the boar's tusk hanging around his neck, shoulder-length hair, and a bow and arrows, he resembled a miniature Tarzan.

He and Truman were out early this summer morning. The hunters were on the prowl; hunted beware.

It had rained a little the past couple of days. Water had accumulated in the low spots, enabling the barefooted boy to move silently along the edges of the lake. Calvin was hoping he might have a shot at a wood duck or two.

They were wading in the bogs on the back side of the lake near the cane break when Truman began barking and pawing the ground. Calvin couldn't see what was in the tall grass, but Truman was circling around something that had him upset. He would stick his head in and then jump back quickly. Calvin thought it might be a snake, so he ran toward Truman, shouting for him to stay back.

Once Calvin got closer, he spotted the most lethal inhabitant in the swamp. Truman was irritating the largest rattlesnake Calvin had ever seen. The snake was coiled and poised, ready to strike. The massive snake was larger than Calvin's thigh at his thickest point. The reptile could kill several men with its venom in one strike.

"Truman, get back! Get back!" Calvin screamed.

The snake would strike, and Truman would retreat just in time to avoid the bite. The dog wasn't used to backing down from anything. Calvin had a sick feeling in his stomach; he knew he would have to kill the snake before Truman would leave it alone. Either the dog or the snake would have to die.

The huge timber rattlesnake had its rattles held high, sounding the warning: "Don't come any closer!"

Since Calvin's arrows were only sharpened sticks and had no stone or metal points, he knew he would have to kill the head. It would have to be a perfect shot; if he missed the head and hit the body, the snake would still strike and perhaps hit Truman.

The snake's heart-shaped head was elevated above his coiled body and was following Truman's every move. One strike from this monster snake, and it would be over.

Calvin moved closer as he drew his arrow, whispered a prayer, and let the arrow fly. It ripped through the serpent's head. The boy trembled with relief but felt like he was going to throw up.

He held Truman back until the snake finally stopped moving. Grabbing the tail, Calvin stretched the snake out, all seven feet of him. He cut the rattles off and put them in his pocket—another trophy to add to his collection.

Calvin drug the snake back to camp, hung it up, and skinned it. He had plans to turn the skin into a headband. Now he had to talk himself into using the meat for food. He hadn't eaten snake of any kind before, and not even Mr. Poole had insisted on it.

He found the meat white and firm. It looked a lot like skinned alligator gar. He had heard rattlesnake was good. Some said it tasted like chicken. Of course it did, and it did. Calvin knew if he was hungry enough, he would eat most anything. It was protein, and it didn't matter what it was or what it tasted like. He was hungry.

He put a spoonful of lard in his skillet, cut the snake in six-inch links, and fried it up. He gave the rest to Truman, who ate it raw.

"Hey, Truman, it does taste like chicken," he said, laughing.

With their stomachs stretched tight with snake meat, they took the rest of the day off. Calvin took a bar of lava soap and a rag and striped down to his birthday suit, same as Truman. They headed to a deep hole on the river and jumped off the bank. It sounded like two bowling balls were thrown into the water. It was cold and took their breath away. They soon grew accustomed to the chilly water. Calvin lathered them both up for a much-needed bath.

Life has its moments, some good, some not. But even though the water was a little chilly, a boy skinny-dipping with his buddy, the best dog in the world, is as good as it gets!

They frolicked there for the rest of the afternoon. Calvin climbed on Truman's back and let the big dog pull him around. He was a powerful animal! They both loved the water and were natural swimmers.

Calvin took the opportunity to check himself, as well as Truman, for ticks. Ticks loved to bury themselves in hard to get to places like ears, on top of your head, and other spots even more remote. If not removed, they could cause an infection.

Completely exhausted, Calvin lay on the bank staring up through the canopy of green leaves at a tapestry of clouds floating in a sea of blue. At that moment, he didn't have a care in the world; it was good to be eleven. There were so many times in his young life when he dreamed of the comfort and protection of this refuge. The fragrance of new foliage and honeysuckle permeated the air. The perpetual movement of the Tensas, on its never-ending journey south, caressed his soul and soothed the wounds he had suffered at such a young age.

The summer breeze and slants of sunlight through the layers of leaves overhead made it too hard for him to keep his eyes open. He succumbed to the weight of his eyelids, and they fell shut. Off in the distance, he could hear Truman splashing along the shallow sand bars. With his eyes closed, he could still follow the noise the dog was making, farther and farther down the river until all was silent.

He wasn't sure if he was awake or dreaming, but Calvin became aware of a sound he hadn't heard in a while. It was the sound of human voices. He refrained from jumping up, but could tell without lifting his head they were upriver and moving in his direction.

Calvin stayed on his back and slowly slid feet first into the water. Without standing, he made his way to an undercut with overhanging roots. He crawled into it and took handfuls of mud covering his head and shoulders. The perfect camouflage, only two eyes were now peering out of the dark water hole.

He had moved thirty or forty feet upriver from where he had first entered. Holding his breath, he was hoping that they wouldn't notice all the tracks and where he slid back into the water. Then suddenly he remembered the bar of soap and the rag he left on the bank, but it was too late. If he tried to get them now, they would see him for sure.

Calvin could hear their low grumblings as they made their way along the riverbank toward him. He was thankful Truman had taken off downriver. He knew if he was there he would confront them.

The foul language that emitted from these two confirmed Calvin's suspicions. They had to be the same two guys he had encountered earlier. Calvin was finally able to get a look at them from the corner of his eye without moving his head. They stumbled into view.

One was short and stocky, with dirty blondish hair that covered his ears, as though someone put a bowl over his head and cut it with a pair of shears. His teeth and hair were the same color. A dark line of snuff ran from the corner of his mouth. His dirty undershirt exposed two red-freckled shoulders, and his arms looked like two tattooed hams. He was carrying something in his right hand. From Calvin's view, he couldn't make out what it was, but in the other hand was a mason jar containing a clear liquid. From the way he was stumbling around, it had to be moonshine!

The other was tall and skinny as a rail, and had a patchy black beard all over his face. Just like the other guy, they both dipped. There was a stream of snuff dripping from the corner of his mouth, and teeth were a scarce commodity.

He was wearing a floppy leather hat and faded overalls with no shirt. A thick growth of black hair was on his chest and back. A long white neck protruded from his hairy shoulders, appearing too small for his head. He was carrying a double-bit ax in one hand, and a crate full of chickens was balanced on his head. The sorry-looking pair were preoccupied with their conversation, which Calvin couldn't hear well enough to understand. But each statement was punctuated with a cuss word that he heard loud and clear. The cussing echoed throughout the swamp and left no doubt this was a couple of bad people whom he shouldn't get involved with.

They were on track to walk right over the bar of soap and rag when the tall one stopped and sniffed the air. He stood there like a bloodhound with his nose in the air and then took a few steps in the direction of the camp. Stopping again, he yelled back at his partner, "Hey, Claude, smells like somebody's smokin' uh hog!"

Just as the chubby guy was about to step on the soap, he turned and walked up the hill to see what the skinny one was yelling about. They huddled together for a moment, discussing their strategy. Then separating, they each started walking toward the camp. One went right and the other left.

The moonshine had taken its toll. The stocky man was having trouble walking. Calvin saw him stumble and fall.

This was his chance. He crawled to the edge of the bank, rubbed mud all over the rest of his body, made a wide circle, and still beat both men to the campsite. Calvin got a glimpse of what the chubby fellow had in the other hand: it was a double-barreled shotgun. Once he saw the camp, he threw the jar of moonshine down and grabbed the gun with both hands.

Calvin arrived seconds ahead of the skinny guy, hid behind a bush, and waited to see what they were up to.

"Hey, Claude, git yer ol' fat ass up here. I done found what wuz smellin' good," the skinny guy yelled. He was standing there, gaping up at the canvas full of smoked pork. "Look at des place. Ain't nobody here. We'll git it all, an' put 'er in dat li'l ol' wagon, yuh kin pull it." He laughed.

Calvin wasn't going to let them take the meat without a fight. He had a plan, but it might just get him shot. Then once again, just in time, he heard Truman running toward him.

"Quiet, boy. Come here," Calvin said as he put a finger to his mouth. He bent down and grabbed him around the neck. Truman was looking at him with his head cocked to the side. Calvin had forgotten the fact he was covered with mud and still didn't have a stitch on. He made the dog stay but wasn't sure what would happen when he saw the two men.

Calvin was within reach of the extra moss he had collected to make the target. He covered himself from head to toe with it and stepped up on a stump. The moss draped all the way to the ground, making him appear eight feet tall.

The men had been drinking and were a little woozy, which made them oblivious to what was going on around them, until Calvin raised his arms and let out a bloodcurdling scream. Calvin looked like something from the Black Lagoon.

The skinny guy was first to get a good look at the eight-foot monster. He jerked the crate off his head and threw it down. The crate broke open, and chickens flew in all directions. He stumbled backward, encouraging his partner to follow.

"Run, Claude, run. Dat dang thang's gone 'a git us!"

The stocky man whirled around and pointed the double-barrel at the swamp monster. Before he could squeeze the triggers, Truman leaped from the ground and was in midair. His huge front paws landed on Claude's chest, causing the gun to discharge both barrels straight up. The big dog straddled him and pinned him to the ground, with his jaws clamped around his neck.

"Let 'em go, boy!" Calvin shouted.

Truman slowly relaxed his grip. The fat man, even though somewhat impaired, sprang to his feet, screaming, "Help! Help! Swamp monster! Run fer yuh life! It's da swamp monster!"

Calvin had to snicker to himself. The short fat man ran wildly through the woods, bouncing off trees like a pinball, pleading for his buddy, Rufus, to wait for him.

CALVIN AND THE GREAT TENSAS RIVER BOTTOM

Calvin picked up the gun, held it by the barrel, spun around a couple of times, and let it go. It landed in the lake. He had no shells and didn't want the gun around.

The image of the two drunken characters, running hysterically through the woods, was amusing. However, he knew this wasn't a laughing matter, because once they sobered up, they would probably be back.

Calvin took a quick dip in the lake to get the mud off. While putting his overalls on, he took a look around and decided there was only one thing they could do.

It took all night to break camp and put everything they could in the cart. He now had a double-bit ax to pack. It would come in handy but was more weight. They had too much for the cart to hold, so Calvin would pull what was left of the smoked pork on the slide. They moved out before the sun was up, leaving their wonderful little place.

This gave him empathy for the nomadic tribes. They were constantly breaking camp and moving. This wasn't easy for Calvin. This had been their first major camp, and he had worked so hard to construct the shelter and smoker. They stopped for one last look at their home for the past two months knowing they would never see it again.

CHAPTER 11

The Featherweight

Even though the going was slow and tiring, Truman seemed to enjoy pulling the cart again. The weather was hot and humid. They stopped often to drink from the canvas water bag. Calvin knew the chances of finding another spring like the one they had were not good. He sat on a log and savored the last of the cool sweet water as he began thinking of the consequences that may arise from the encounter with the two hooligans.

He had an uneasy feeling knowing that, once those two got back home, there's no telling what they would conjure up. They may have folks looking for an eight-foot mossy-covered monster with a larger-than-life rabid dog. Perhaps others would come looking for him. He would just have to keep moving deeper into the swamp; that's all he could do.

While pondering his dilemma, he had picked up a stick and was using it to dig around in the leaves on the ground. Out of nowhere, a small copper-colored hen appeared and began to scratch in the same leaf pile. Calvin couldn't believe his eyes. There was a perfect diminutive chicken, pecking at the mud between his toes.

The prissy little bantam hen talked to herself as she scratched for bugs and worms in the leaves. She hopped up on the log beside him. From there, she continued to hop to his knee, and next thing he knew, she was sitting on his shoulder. Calvin held out his arm. With no hesitation and in one hop, she was perched on his arm.

He was delighted with their new guest. Truman took little notice until she flew from Calvin's arm to his back. For once, this noble canine was a little humiliated as she walked sideways, step by step, until she was atop his head. Calvin's laugher didn't help the situation.

She made herself at home, hopping from place to place, checking out the slide with the smoked pork and then the cart. Calvin was impressed with her agility. She seemed to be everywhere at once. She even flew to the top of a tree and looked down at the little expedition.

After observing her for a while, he knew she had no intention of wandering off, and she needed a name. Calvin shouted, "Hey, your name is Penny. Her name is Penny, Truman, because she's thu color of uh penny!"

The little bantam hen had followed them all morning. They probably would never know why the two ne'er-do-wells had a crate full of chickens or why she chose to follow the cart; but, as time went by, they would become most grateful.

It was noon, and they hadn't had anything to eat. Calvin took a ham and cut some strips off for him and Truman. He shaved some of the smoked caramelized skin for Penny. She seemed most grateful and made sure she wasn't left behind when Calvin gave Truman the move-out whistle.

The little hen hopped up on the tongue of the cart and slipped inside. There was barely enough room for her to squeeze under the canvas top. Calvin thought this was odd, but if she wanted to ride inside, that was fine with him.

They proceeded with no particular destination in mind, just trying to put some distance between them and the old campsite. They traveled within sight of the river but weren't trying to follow the bank. He had hopes of finding another lake similar to the one they had left behind—especially one with a spring close by. This wouldn't be likely, but they would do the best they could. Chances were, they could find a lake with no spring or find spring with no lake, but probably not both. If they kept moving, it was possible to travel six more miles before nightfall.

Calvin had noticed that the May haws were getting ripe. They were mostly used for making jelly but were eatable right off the tree. They would provide fruit for his diet, and he was looking forward to having some for supper. He would try to find a place that had a grove of May haw trees to spend the night.

Calvin couldn't wait to jump in the river this afternoon. There was still mud in his hair and ears. The quick sponge bath in the lake hadn't removed it all, and it was beginning to irritate him.

Their travel was slow. Calvin's arms were cramping, and he would have to stop and rest. Sometimes, the slide would get wedged between trees, and he would stop and wrestle it out. Truman would slow down and wait on him to catch up. He showed great patience but pulled his cargo with little effort and seemed to wonder what Calvin's problem was.

They had stopped to rest when Penny began to cackle inside the cart. She hopped out on the tongue, cackled more, and stuck her head back inside. Calvin was curious about her actions. He pulled the canvas back, reached inside, and took out a little warm brown egg.

"Wow, that's great! Look at this, Truman," he said, holding it up. He hadn't eaten an egg since the Canein' Man had made breakfast behind the old store.

Calvin wondered how often she would lay an egg. Once a day or once a week, he had no idea. But no matter how often it would be, any egg would surely be welcomed. Penny would be a valuable addition to their survival.

Once Penny saw that Calvin had found her prize, she hopped from the cart onto Truman's back, walking step by step sideways until she was on top of his head. Calvin couldn't help but laugh a little, because Truman always carried himself with such a noble air. Now for reasons only known to him, Truman tolerated the indignity of having a chicken sitting on his head. However, Calvin noticed a side benefit as they walked along.

Penny began checking out the dog's ears and head for ticks. She was busy as a bee until satisfied all was clear. She flew to the ground and began filling her crop with the bounties from the bug-infested swamp. Calvin was pleased to see she was self-sufficient. It was certainly hard enough to keep him and Truman fed.

When Truman wasn't pulling the cart, he would scavenge the swamp in order to provide some of his own food. Penny, on the other hand, not only could feed herself but could also contribute an egg from time to time. She would make a great addition to the team.

Penny scratched around in the damp leaves for insects and worms as they moved slowly along. She had no problem keeping up.

Calvin struggled to keep the slide from getting hung on cypress knees and logs. The ground was soft, making travel more difficult. They had to cross muddy flats and sloughs filled with water, preventing them from making much progress. Calvin used his machete to clean mud from the cart wheels and occasionally opened a path for their little caravan. This was hard work for Calvin, but Truman pulled the cart with little effort.

Exhausted, he decided to start looking for a place with May haw trees close by and set up camp for the night.

May haws are found in swampy areas throughout the south. They ripen in the spring, then fall from the small trees and cover the ground. Just about all the wildlife in the swamp love the reddish-orange-colored fruit. It's a special favorite of deer and wild hogs.

May haws are about the same size and look similar to crab apples. Most people don't eat them raw, but cook them down to make jelly. Calvin would take really ripe ones and suck the juice; it was protein and tasted great to him. He was able to pick up a few as they moved along, keeping his mind off the hard task of pulling the slide.

Calvin had the river on his left and several small sloughs on his right. The idea was to keep moving south. He finally spotted a nice grove of May haw trees. It wasn't the perfect site for a camp, but at least he would have a chance to gather several buckets of May haws before dark.

Calvin's legs had become rubbery from pulling the slide. After unhitching Truman, he collapsed in a heap on the ground. He watched with amazement as the superdog trotted off to explore the new campsite. He was completely spent, but Truman wasn't even breathing hard. Penny stayed nearby, scratching herself up a little supper. Calvin was worn to the bone but couldn't resist the thought of a dip in the cool water of the Tensas River.

It didn't take long for his young body to be rejuvenated from the soak in the river. He set up camp and began to gather May haws. The great thing about this particular fruit is its abundance this time of year. Calvin would cook them down and sprinkle a little sugar on them. Everything tasted better with a little May haw marmalade.

The art of survival is to take advantage of what is available at the moment and can be obtained with the least amount of energy. There are a lot of food sources to be had in the swamp but at different seasons and in various quantities. Calvin knew if he had to burn more calories finding food than he got from eating it, he hadn't accomplished anything.

Mr. Poole had shown him that palmetto roots were edible but required a lot of digging, and they have very little protein. It was the same with cattail roots. These you would consider only when there was nothing else that required less effort.

It was already getting late, and he was too tired to do anything with the camp other than start a fire. He put the May haws that were overripe in the skillet, covered them with sugar, and placed it on the coals. They made tasty syrup-like dessert. He would have a little of the smoked ham with it.

Calvin sat by the campfire and was pleased when Penny joined him. He had a handful of May haws for her. She pecked at them from his hand. He placed them on the ground, and the two enjoyed their supper without Truman's company.

The last time Calvin saw him, he was splashing along the river's edge. He was heading south for places unknown and probably wouldn't be back until morning. Calvin gathered palmetto palms and covered them with moss for a bed. Mosquitoes were going to be bad tonight, so he put on his socks and long handles. He put wet green moss on the coals, hoping the smoke would help keep the insects away.

Lying on his pallet, staring up at the sky, he was somewhat surprised when Penny flew from the ground to a tree limb just above his head to roost. He watched her dark silhouette against the sky as she preened her feathers, stretched her legs, and then settled down for the night. She placed herself there for the purpose of a visual vantage point. She would be able to see any movement from all directions.

Calvin was so grateful for this little puff of feathers. Like Truman, she seemed just to appear from nowhere. Now he wondered what he would have done without them. Who could have known she would become his watchdog when the top dog was out on the prowl.

The sky slowly darkened until he could no longer see Penny, but just knowing she was there and would let him know if anything approached was comforting.

The night revealed thousands of stars sprinkled across their view. The anticipation of rain caused insects, birds, and especially frogs of all kinds, big and small, to fill the swamp with their song. Calvin had become accustomed to this serenade, and now it would be hard to sleep without it.

All of a sudden, Truman came running through the brush, making a lot of noise, disturbing Penny. Being irritated, she started cackling, scolding the big dog. She had only been with them a short while but literally ruled the roost.

Calvin was now wide awake, and he knew it would be a long hard day setting up camp tomorrow.

"Bad dog, where have yuh been?" he asked under his breath. "What uh couple of characters I have for companions," he said, smiling to himself.

Truman curled up beside him. Penny settled back down on her roost, and the three drifted off to sleep. Before the sun broke the horizon, Penny dropped from her perch, almost hitting Calvin on the head. He knew it probably was not an accident.

"That pint-size chicken is uh mess," he grunted.

He sat up rubbing sleep from his eyes but then thought about his little egg, and all was forgiven. He looked around for Truman. He was nowhere to be seen. This was a good thing, because the egg was much too small to share.

Calvin put the frying pan on the hot coals with some smoked pork, and the May haw marmalade. He cracked the egg on the side, sunny-side up. Even Mr. Poole would be proud of this survivalist breakfast!

Breakfast was small but tasty. What Calvin wanted to know most of all was when he would get another egg. Calvin gave Penny a handful of May haws. Now that breakfast was over, he had to find a good water source. Water is the most important item for survival!

Truman was still gone. Calvin thought he heard him bark once. He very seldom barked, and if he did, it was for a reason. Either he was in hot pursuit of a rabbit, or he had treed a squirrel. Calvin could always tell the difference. If he was actually trying to catch something, he would make a little yelping sound as he ran. This sounded as if he was getting close to providing his own breakfast this morning.

While Truman was on the hunt, Calvin needed to find a water source. This shouldn't be a problem. He could always dig a hole on a sandbar, and it would fill overnight, as water seeps in from the river. He would rather not have to pack water up the bank, which would require too much energy. A small stream running from a slough into the river, or hopefully a spring, would be a much better option.

Once he had established his water source, he would decide where to make camp and how much effort to put into it. After the May haws were gone, if fishing and hunting wasn't that good, he would move on. He decided not to make a shelter; he would just sleep on the ground or in the cart if it rained.

Calvin grabbed his bow and headed for the river. While looking for spring water, he might see a bullfrog or two. He prided himself on moving quietly through the woods as the Indians were known to do. However, as usual, Truman heard him and came running. Calvin could tell by his full stomach he had breakfast already.

"Hey, boy, where yuh been?" Truman ran up to Calvin and stuck his wet nose on his bare chest for a pat on the head. "What'd yuh catch, uh rabbit?"

He knew if Truman had caught a rabbit, it was not an easy feat for a dog his size or a dog of any size for that matter. A rabbit was just too agile. He probably ran him into a stump hole and dug him out, thought Calvin. Whatever it was by the look of his stomach, he wouldn't have to eat for a couple of days.

Calvin got back to looking for water. It didn't take long before he found a small stream, trickling down the riverbank. The water was clear and tasted good enough, not as good as the spring. At least he wouldn't have to climb the riverbank with a bucket of water several times a day.

With the water problem solved, he decided to hold off building a lean-to. He wasn't sure how long they would stay at this location. He could always build one later if the hunting and fishing proved to be worth it.

Calvin spent the next few days making the camp as comfortable as possible without going to the effort of building a waterproof shelter. He decided to construct a simple shade by leaning poles against a cross pole in the forks of two small trees and covering them with palmetto palms. This would provide shade but wouldn't keep them completely dry if it rained. A little rain wouldn't hurt the animals, and he could sleep in the cart.

Another necessity was a good supply of firewood. He looked for logs that had washed downriver from previous floods, and from the looks of things, there had been a lot of floods. He had noticed the water marks and other debris lodged in trees around the camp. It was frightening because some were about ten feet above his head. If they were close to the river when it flooded, they would be in great danger.

Calvin had given this a lot of thought. He knew the odds were not in his favor. At some point, with a heavy rain, the water would rise above the banks. They would be trapped with no way out. He would have to come up with a way to survive a major flood.

CHAPTER 12

The Motor Boat

The new campsite was working but didn't compare to the oxbow camp. After a change in the weather and some light showers, fishing was only fair. Calvin decided to concentrate on hunting. He knew frog gigging should be excellent. The bellowing sound they made were deafening at night, and that's why they were called bullfrogs. They sounded like a bull bellowing. The sloughs were full of them, so he planned to thin out their population a little and fry some frog legs.

Calvin had killed birds and squirrels with his bow and arrow, but a personal goal was to hit a duck in flight. He had been told that was one of the responsibilities of young Indian boys his age—hunting small game and waterfowl with a bow. They were able to hit ducks in flight. Calvin thought this to be the ultimate challenge.

Wood ducks lived in the Tensas River Bottom year-round. Most didn't migrate like other ducks. Calvin would often see them early in the morning as they left their roost. Then just at dark, they returned.

Calvin was slipping along the edge of a slough in a heavy fog. He could hear the shrill call of wood ducks, as they left their roost. Locals referred to them as squealers, because their sound is more like a squeal than a quack. He quietly slipped into the shallow slough and crouched with his bow and arrow behind a grove of tupelo gum.

Woodies don't respond to decoys very well. Calvin didn't have any, anyway. His hope was to be in the right place at the right time. He held his breath as he watched several woodies break through the thick fog.

With their wings cupped and feet dropped, they landed in the opening in front of him and swam in his direction. Calvin waited until he was comfortable with the shot and drew his bow; and, with a thump, the closest one was floating upside down in the slough while the others jumped straight up.

He placed another arrow on his bow and, with one smooth motion, followed a duck in flight, then pulled past his head and released the arrow. To his great surprise, the duck collapsed in an explosion of feathers and fell headfirst with a splash of water.

He was so excited. He did his version of a war dance, jumping up and down whooping, hollering, and splashing water everywhere.

"I'm uh Indian. I can hit ducks on thu wing!" he shouted. And there again, no one witnessed his accomplishment, except for Truman, who came running over to see what all the hollering was about.

"Did yuh see that, big boy?"

Truman just looked at him with his head cocked to the side. Calvin knew it was probably luck. Chances were, he may not be able to do it again, but be that as it may, he was going to roast ducks over the campfire tonight. That made him happy.

The three settled into their routine, which was trying to find enough food to get them through the day. There was very little of the pork left. Calvin had taken the ham and shoulder bones cracked them open with his hatchet and shared the marrow with Penny and Truman. He used the bones to make soup. Nothing was wasted, but now that it was gone, they would need to find food every day.

Fishing with a cane pole isn't always productive. Unfortunately, small game could be hunted out quickly, near the campsite. Subsistence hunting required them to travel farther and farther from the camp to find food. May haw season was coming to a close, and they were getting harder to find.

It was late afternoon; Calvin and Truman were on their way back to camp. He had managed to bag a couple of bullfrogs while wadding the sloughs. Even they were getting harder to find. There were only a few hours of light, so he walked the trail along the riverbank. He could follow it back to camp even in the dark.

Suddenly, Truman stopped, and the hair stiffened on his back. The dog was watching something on the river as he made a low growling sound. The whine from a boat motor broke the silence of the swamp.

All the times he and Mr. Poole came to this river, he never remembered seeing a boat with a motor on it. Folks used paddles and small flat bottom boats or pirogues. What made this so strange was this was the second time in the last few days he had heard an outboard motor on the Tensas. There weren't many folks who owned one, and the Tensas wasn't a river for joyriding anyway. There were too many stumps and logs.

They hid behind a bush and waited until the boat rounded the bend in the river. To Calvin's surprise, he saw a large flat bottom boat and six men in it all carrying shotguns. Scanning the riverbank, they were talking quietly as they pointed in all directions and looked as if their heads were on swivels.

There was a guy wearing a khaki shirt and pants. With a strawhat sitting squarely on his head, Calvin knew even before he saw the tin star that he was in charge. They were right beneath the steep bank now, and Calvin could see them plainly from the waist up. He couldn't believe his eyes. There was the tall skinny character who tried to rob him.

They shut the motor off, and the sheriff stood up in the boat. "Rufus, I don't think yuh know what you're talking 'bout. You an' yuh ol' buddy, fat boy Claude, were too full of moonshine. You were probably hallucinating, an' even if yuh did see somethin', yuh can't remember where yuh were when yuh saw it," said the sheriff.

"Where is Claude anyway? Didn't I let him out uh jail before we left? That knucklehead was supposed ta come with us." The other men all laughed. "He's the only one that had uh mark on'im. Where's that giant dog that had'im by the throat?" he asked.

"Yeah, yuh let'im out, but it wasn't thu big ol' dog dat scarred 'im so bad. It wuz de swamp monster! He said he ain't never gone 'a come back in des swamp thu rest of his life," said Rufus.

"We might uh'been a li'l tipsy, but we both seen 'im! Like I said, it wuz 'bout eight foot tall, with dried black mud on its face, with what looked like moss or grayish hair all over 'im."

When he said that, every man in the boat tightened his grip on their shotgun and began nervously scanning the riverbanks.

"Listen, I told yuh thu only reason I agreed ta come back out here was ta look one more time for that runaway boy," said the sheriff. "I don't believe any of this garbage 'bout monsters an' giant dogs."

"But, Sheriff, it's da truth. I saw it with my own eyes," said Rufus.

"Well, so far, yuh been completely worthless. Yuh can't even find thu campsite where yuh thought thu boy camped. I'm telling yuh, there ain't no way uh eleven-year-old boy could survive in this swamp. I don't think he's still alive. I told everybody 'bout seeing one of his overall straps hanging on uh log below thu bridge," said the sheriff.

"Yeah, but what uh 'bout thu wagon tracks?" asked a guy from the back of the boat.

"That don't mean nothin'. It had rained so much I couldn't tell whether it was coming or going. We don't know for sure that boy had anything ta do with them tracks. I'm gone uh say it again. Thu only thing I know for sure, there just ain't no way that boy could survive out here by himself."

"Rufus, don't look at me like that. So yuh say yuh saw thu wagon, but yuh ain't produced no wagon, an' you shor ain't produced no swamp monster," said the sheriff.

"Everybody's heard thu stories 'bout monsters in thu swamps, but you an' yuh old booze-headed buddy Claude are thu only two characters I've ever known that actually claims they seen him," laughed the sheriff.

"I tell yuh, we done gone too fer downriver," said Rufus. "We passed whar thu camp wuz 'bout uh mile back."

"Well, that's too bad 'cause we're going all thu way down to thu fish camp," said the sheriff. "We'll see if ol' black Preacher Joe has seen or heard anything. He'll be at that fish shack this time of year, and nuthin' gets by him. We'll spend thu night somewhere on thu bank, then head on down in thu morning," said the sheriff.

"Dat's gotta be six or eight miles from here, and it looks like its gone'uh rain," hollered one of the men in the back of the boat.

"Shut up! I don't care how far it is!" shouted the sheriff. "We've got'a tent! This is the last time I'm coming out here looking for that boy. I'm tired of folks telling me I ain't doin' my job. This is thu third trip ta this swamp, an' it's goin' ta be thu last, whether I find 'im or not," the sheriff said, sounding exasperated.

Calvin was terrified at what he was hearing. He knew if they were found, the sheriff would take him back, and he had no idea what would happen to Truman. But, regardless, that was the funniest conversation he had ever heard, and to think they were responsible for it all. As soon as they started the outboard, he and Truman ran toward the camp.

He was surprised to see Penny running up from behind them, neck stretched out and feathers all ruffled. She would run some and then fly a few yards but managed to stay up with them. Calvin figured she must have perched in a tree and watched the whole thing. There was no time to lose. They had to pack up and leave immediately.

One good thing was Calvin didn't have to pull a slide full of smoked pork. One bad thing was there was no more smoked pork. There were only a couple of bones left for Truman with very little meat on them. They had the two frogs, and Calvin had saved six of Penny's eggs. He now knew she laid an egg every other day. They were small, so he saved them until he had enough to scramble with some wild onions or whatever he could find to add a little flavor. But for now they would have to work on empty stomachs.

He needed to take down the shelter so it wouldn't be obvious if the men came looking for it. If he worked quickly, they could put a couple of miles between them and the old campsite before it was too dark to travel.

He leveled the shelter and packed everything in the cart, and they struck out downriver. They would follow the river so he could hear the motor if they changed their minds and decided to come back tonight.

They made good time because Calvin wasn't pulling the heavy slide. Still he was exhausted from breaking camp. He finally grabbed Truman's harness.

"This is far enough for now, boy," he said, out of breath.

Penny hopped off his back and started scratching around, looking for a little supper. Calvin took his last box of matches and hurriedly made a small fire. He skinned the frogs and put them on sticks to roast. Two frogs weren't much of a meal, and he was still hungry, but that's all there was. He was saving the eggs for breakfast.

He gave Truman all the frog trimmings—the skin, intestines, and heads. He also gave him the pork bones. The big dog lay down by the fire and with his powerful jaws began grinding every morsel of meat and marrow from them. It was a meager meal, but it would have to do.

Calvin took the small canvas and laid it on the ground next to the fire. He had noticed a change in the weather. Dark rolling clouds were moving in from the northwest, dropping the temperature and making the fire feel especially good. He took his quilt from the cart, wrapped it around his shoulders, sat by the fire like an Indian, and watched the storm build up.

There was nothing like sitting by the fire and feeling the darkness close in around him. He often thought of early man and his ability to make fire. This separated him from all other inhabitants on earth. Fire allowed Homo sapiens to live in environments colder than they otherwise could.

Calvin had always loved the smell of leaves burning. It was the smoke. He knew smoke was sacred to the Indians because it was a by-product of fire. Fire gave them life. In prehistoric times, all humanity and everything they owned smelled like smoke.

The smell of smoke suddenly changed to the smell of rain. It caught him unprepared. He feared he would probably get wet tonight. Taking everything out of the cart in order to sleep wasn't a good option. The only thing he retrieved was the bucket, which he placed under the edge of the cart to catch water when it started to rain.

Calvin cut a short pole just long enough to hold the canvas over his head. For the moment, sitting by the fire and listening to the low rumbling of thunder was most pleasant. He watched the silent flickering glow of electricity, lighting up the clouds and then fading dark again. It was mesmerizing.

He was alone for the moment and, as usual, began thinking of events that brought him to sitting on the ground, in the middle of a dark snake-infested swamp.

He missed his little sister and tried not to think about her. Self-pity wasn't a luxury he could afford. Tonight, for whatever reason, he began thinking about not only Emily Mae but his deceased mother and missing father.

Calvin knew he would never see his mother this side of heaven, but he still had hopes that one day his father would come home and find him. There were times when he thought he saw a figure moving through the dark shadows in the evening light. His first thought was that maybe it was his daddy coming for him, but the image would fade quickly, and then he wasn't sure he had seen anything at all.

He lay back on one elbow to watch the lightning in the distance and soon fell asleep. Calvin woke abruptly with a loud clap of thunder and a flash of lightning as it struck a nearby tree. The smell of sulfur hung in the air, and the hair on his arms stood straight up. It was so bright he could see everything around him perfectly clear.

Truman came running from the dark woods into the light, looking for Calvin's protection. Penny bailed from her roost, hit the ground, and frantically tried to worm her way inside the cart. When that failed, she scampered underneath. She clearly had her feathers ruffled.

Calvin was a little amused. Both his companions, who usually make a point to portray such self-control, had just fallen apart in the presence of Mother Nature's wrath. Calvin chuckled, feeling somewhat superior to his animal friends who seemed to have overreacted to a little thunder and lightning.

The amusement didn't last long, however. The next thing he knew, the dark clouds opened up, and sheets of water pounded the ground. Calvin grabbed the tentpole, pushed it under the canvas, and at the same time stuck the other end in the ground. He crawled underneath and wrapped himself in the quilt.

Truman was determined to get his 140-pound body under the small tent with Calvin, bringing with him that lovely wet-dog smell. Now they were both wet. Calvin gladly shared his small accommodations with Truman, and with every pop of lightning, he tightened his hold on the big dog. That was all he could do, and he hoped it would soon pass. He knew it was going to be a miserable night. Finally, the violent thunder and lightning slowly diminished until it was only a distant rumble. Only an occasional pale flash flickered as the storm slowly moved north. The rain continued.

Early the next morning, Calvin realized he was alone. He was also cold, wet, and could barely uncoil from the fetal position he had lay in for hours in an attempt to stay warm. He lifted the tarp and looked around. Water was everywhere. Trenches of runoff were making its way toward the river. There were no coals left on the fire.

Water had seeped under the canvas and soaked his blanket. He made a quick survey of the situation; it was going to be extremely difficult for Truman to pull the cart, especially since he was nowhere to be seen.

Penny had also left her shelter underneath the cart. Calvin had been abandoned sometime during the night. There was little he could do for his fellow travelers, and at the moment he needed a fire and some dry clothes. There was still a light mist, and with no coals, it was going to be a chore to get a fire started.

He spotted a large pin oak that had been blown over sometime in the past. This would possibly provide a dry surface. However, starting one might still be the problem if he couldn't find enough dry kindling.

Calvin left the wet quilt under the makeshift tent and waded barefooted in black delta mud to the cart. He was wearing his overalls without a shirt. He never wore his brogans anymore. They were much too small, even with the toes cut out.

Just as he stuck his head inside, he heard a gunshot. Calvin froze in place for a moment, listening for another shot, but there wasn't one. He thought it was probably the sheriff and his boys heading back upriver having a mess of cat squirrels for breakfast.

"Set down, Rufus," hollered the sheriff, "Your staggering around like that will either swamp thu boat, or yuh gone 'a fall out."

"I got 'a go, Sheriff. Dat's all is to it," said Rufus with a strained voice.

"The current's too swift right here. Wait'l we come ta thu wider place in thu river, an' we'll try ta ease over ta thu bank. I speck everybody's got'uh go," said the sheriff.

One of the boys grabbed hold of a cypress limb. The motor was shut off, and all hands were needed to get the bow of the large john boat on the slippery wet bank. After tying it to a log so the swift current wouldn't wash it back downstream, they bailed out in all directions. They were all looking for the perfect bush that would afford a little privacy.

Rufus took the lead, running with his shotgun in one hand while trying to unbuckle his overall straps with the other. Finally, he squatted with great relief behind a big clump of palmetto palms.

He propped his gun against a nearby tree and began scanning the area for perfect leaves. He suddenly caught a glimpse of a large dark object moving in a mass of palmetto a few yards away. Thinking it might be a big black bear, he reached for his gun, fired off a shot from the hip, and at the same time felt a swat to the side of his head. Everything went dark as his face hit the damp ground.

The sheriff and the other boys heard the gunshot and came running.

"What thu hell are yuh shootin' at?" shouted the sheriff as they got closer. Rufus was gaining consciousness and trying to sit up when the sheriff, along with several of the boys, came running toward him.

"Rufus, did yuh shoot yuhself?" asked the youngest and fastest of the group as he placed a hand on his shoulder, trying to steady him.

Rufus was on his knees, staring into space while rubbing the back of his neck.

Finally, the sheriff reached the scene, holding his side all bent over and out of breath. He placed his hands on his knees and when he could finally speak, shouted, "What're yuh shootin' at, yuh idiot?"

Rufus, still unable to focus, could hear people talking. They seemed to be only making sounds and not speaking words.

"Look 'uh here, Sheriff. Dar's uh big knot on de side of his head," said one of the boys.

"What happened ta yuh?" asked the sheriff as he tilted Rufus's head back on his spindly neck, for a better look. The big knot was now turning several shades of purple. "Does somebody have uh canteen with 'em? Give this man some water. Stand up an' pull up yuh overalls, Rufus," said the sheriff.

Rufus grabbed the bib of his overalls with the assistance of a couple of boys. There were a few snickers from the spectators as Rufus held the bib in place. Unfortunately, the back door was still wide open.

"Get 'im buckled up, an' help 'im over ta that log," said the sheriff.

"I thank I'm feelin' a li'l better now, Sheriff," said Rufus.

"Tell me what happened then, and for thu last time, what were yuh shootin' at?" asked the sheriff.

"Well, I wuz doin' my business over dar behind them palmetto bushes, when I thought I seen uh big ol' bear, couldn't tell fer shor. It wuz uh dark color thou," said Rufus.

"I grabbed my twelve gauge, loaded wid buckshot, an' fired it at sump tin' moving in thu bushes. I think I mus'ta hit 'im, 'cause I heard him holler. Thu next thang I knowed, it felted like somebody went upside my head. I guess I wuz knocked out cold," he said with a sheepish look on his face.

The sheriff didn't speak for a moment; he just slowly shook his head.

"Yuh see that's what I'm talkin' 'bout Rufus—you an' yuh ol' buddy Claude can't be trusted. Yuh just can't go round shootin'. That could've been one of us in them bushes, Rufus! You might've killed somebody. Get back in thu boat. I'm goin' back ta Tallulah with or without yawl an' ain't coming back. I'm sorry 'bout thu boy. I hope he's still alive, but I doubt it. If I lose my job 'cause I come back without him, so be it, but I've had it," said the exasperated sheriff.

The box of matches were wrapped and stuffed inside one of his coat pockets. He had hurriedly packed all his other stuff on top of his coat last night. Somehow, he would have to get to the matches without taking everything out. Other than the log, there wasn't a dry place in sight.

It hadn't been cold when he climbed under the canvas, so he had left his coat inside the cart. He could carry everything from the cart to the log or try to pull the cart to the log. Neither would be easy.

He decided to unload just enough to get to his coat by stacking things on top of the cart. He carried the last of the kitchen matches, some cotton balls that were coated with Vaseline, and his hatchet to the log.

Calvin took the hatchet and chopped around the inside of hollow logs, looking for anything that was dry enough to burn. With the Vaseline-soaked cotton balls, he should be able to get a fire started unless the matches were too damp. He put his coat on while standing in water. He was shaking so much that gathering wood was difficult.

Finally, he had an armload of kindling. Hopefully, it would be dry enough to burn. He shaved off a flat area on the log with his hatchet, carefully placed the dry material in the middle, and used the limbs to form a small tepee shape around it. He was ready, but there was one major problem. Calvin knew there were only a couple of matches left. If they were too damp to strike, he would have to go back to the cart and get his fire starter bow, which Mr. Poole had helped him make. He had used it successfully to start a fire several times but never under these conditions.

The mist of rain was light but steady. His hands were wet, and now the once-dry material was exposed to the rain. He shook the box close to his ear and could tell there were only a few matches left. The bigger problem was that his hands were wet, and now the box was damp.

He slid the box lid open. With cold trembling fingers, which felt too large for his hands, he took out one of the three matches. Calvin struck the match against the abrasive strip on the side of the box, and the head of the match crumbled without a spark. The result was the same for the other two. With the failure of the last match to strike, Calvin felt a wave of anxiety as cold and hunger ravaged his body.

He planned to scramble Penny's eggs if he could ever get a fire started. Without a fire and food in his cold wet body, hypothermia was a possibility, even though it was a spring day with the temperature in the sixties.

The day was dark and gray, and now a steady rain was falling with no chance of the sun warming things up anytime soon. Calvin sloshed through mud and water once again to retrieve his fire bow.

He placed the cotton balls on a thin piece of cypress board with a hole cut halfway through. He put the stick in the indention, wrapped the bowstring around it, and began to spin it back and forth. He collected the hot cinders, created by friction, and laid the cotton balls on top of them and blew. The alcohol in the Vaseline ignited the cotton swiftly.

Calvin flushed with excitement. He placed the small flame on the scraped area of the log and held his breath as he applied a layer of kindling. If it was still too damp and the fire wouldn't start, then he wouldn't get warm, and there would be no scrambled eggs.

There was a puff of smoke, but as the cotton balls were consumed, the flame slowly disappeared and, along with it, Calvin's hope of warmth and food. The wood he collected was now just too wet. Until the sun came out and dried things, Calvin would be cold and hungry. The only thing he could do was put his dry clothes on and hope the rain would stop.

Today, he learned a valuable lesson he would never forget. From now on, he would pay more attention to the weather and try to be better prepared. He realized how quickly things can change and how dangerous they can become. He was caught off guard. The nights had been warm and humid for the last few weeks, but now he was so cold he could barely function.

Calvin put his dry clothes on and spread the wet ones out on the log to dry, when the sun came out. Devastated that he couldn't get the damp wood to burn, he trudged once again to the cart and managed to move things around enough to crawl inside. At least he was out of the rain and wind. He would just have to hunker down and wait it out. Even when Truman returned, it would still be too wet for him to pull the cart. It might take a couple of days to dry out enough for that.

Inside his little shelter, Calvin could finally feel his core temperature begin to rise. He was exhausted from the ordeal he had gone through and getting little sleep the night before. Calvin curled up inside the cart with the rain and wind pelting the canvas. He went to sleep dreaming of scrambled eggs.

He woke with a start. Calvin didn't know where he was, why he was there, or what was trying to scratch its way inside the canvas flaps.

Penny managed to hop up on the back of the cart, turn her head to the side, and get one leg inside. She was scratching like crazy to get the other under the flap. "What are yuh doing, yuh silly bird?" asked Calvin as he untied the bottom lash.

It was cramped inside even for a small boy, because it wasn't completely empty. Somehow the little hen managed to get in and seemed perfectly content with the close quarters. Calvin untied the other two lashes and was greeted with clear skies.

He left Penny in the cart and hopped out. The ground was covered with water and cold to his bare feet. He grabbed the fire bow and a handful of cotton balls. After several attempts, things had dried out just enough for the fire to start.

Calvin cracked the eggs one at a time on the side of his cast-iron skillet and used his fork to fluff up a pile of golden protein, thanks to Penny. He scrambled up all six precious nuggets and was ready to devour them, when Penny's cackling proclaimed the arrival of number seven. With her usual lack of modesty, Penny hopped from the cart and strutted around looking for praise.

Calvin hungrily scarfed down the eggs and could have eaten that many more. He fetched the latest arrival, cracked it by dropping it whole in the pan, stirring together, shells and all. He heard chickens would sometimes eat their own eggs, if they were missing something in their diet or needed gravel for their crop. He was a little uncomfortable feeding Penny her own egg. It was somewhat akin to cannibalism, he thought. He knew she was hungry. She had provided him with life-sustaining protein, so that was the least he could do for her. Penny consumed the omelet in short order and pecked around long after it was gone.

Immediately after Calvin finished eating, his thoughts returned to Truman. Maybe he was hunting. He hoped he was successful because there was nothing to offer him when he returned.

The cool weather and rain would make fishing almost impossible for several days. There was too much runoff, making the water muddy. Hunting for small game—birds, frogs, turtles, and anything he could find—was his only alternative.

With this much water on the ground, crawfish would make mud stacks. Though it would take time, he might be able to fish them out of their hole with a string and a little bait. He really wanted to put fish traps in the river, but was afraid of being seen when the sheriff and his boys headed back home.

Calvin needed to get more distance between him and the old campsite, but until Truman returned, he was stuck there. No matter that it was wet and muddy, it was getting late. If he wanted to eat tomorrow, he had better start hunting.

Morning found Calvin putting wood on the fire. There were still hot coals when he woke, and it had warmed up some, but he wouldn't let it go out again if there was anyway he could avoid it.

He had a couple dozen crawfish in his bucket, along with salt, black pepper, and just enough water to make a steam. It was all he had to show for his efforts yesterday afternoon. Calvin ate the crawfish tails and gave Penny the heads and shells. He was determined to be a better provider, but without Truman, hunting was much more difficult.

Calvin was worried. Truman had stayed away overnight before, but to be out in a storm didn't make sense to him. He should have come back by now. He took his bow and covered as much ground as he possibly could. Calvin looked for his dog and food at the same time. He decided not to call Truman, because he wasn't sure where his pursuers were and was afraid they might hear him.

By late afternoon, Calvin was exhausted. He had covered a lot of ground. Everything was still wet and muddy, which made walking difficult. Many of the sloughs and low areas were still overflowing with water. There was no sign of Truman. His tracks had been washed away by the rain. Dejected, he gave up and started back to camp.

Calvin hadn't put a lot of effort into finding food, because of his concern for Truman. He had nothing to eat at this point. His hunger reached a point of desperation, but then he saw edible saw palmetto berries everywhere. It was an easy decision. He had managed to avoid them thus far, but this would be the afternoon to give the palmetto a try.

Back at the foster home, Mr. Poole had insisted he try the berries, as well as the stems and roots. He said "the early people" made both a major part of their diet. The berries could be used for medical purposes, as well as for food.

Calvin considered the berries to be among the worst things he ever put in his mouth. However, the stems weren't too bad. The point where they were pulled from the stalks actually provided a couple of tasty bites. The harvesting of the stems would require some effort, but there was no limit to the supply. He planned to boil them with salt and pepper.

Calvin remembered Mr. Poole would often talk about starvation and the eating of saw palmetto berries. The story was from an old book written by Jonathan Dickinson. It was about shipwrecked Quakers off the Florida peninsula during a hurricane in 1696.

According to him, the Quakers were captured by the Jaeger Indian tribe. Unfortunately for the Quakers, they just happened to be cannibals, who would only eat people they didn't know. Again it was unfortunate for the Quakers; they fit the qualifications for becoming the main course for one of their banquets.

The Indians offered the survivors nothing but fish and palmetto berries. The fish they ate but couldn't suffer the taste of the berries. Not only did they hate the berries, they were afraid they were being used to fatten them up for the boiling pot.

Dickinson tells of the chief being brought a basket of palmetto berries while sitting cross legged on the floor of his hut in front of the captives. He ate them greedily and seemed to relish them. But even though the Quakers were starving, they were unable to keep them down.

They described the berries' taste as something liking to the taste of rotten cheese steeped in tobacco juice. Dickinson claimed the Quakers were finally able to tolerate the irksome berry, and most survived their ordeal.

Calvin had put the palmetto berries in the last resort category. He began gathering stems but also gathered a few berries to see if Penny would eat them. This wasn't going to be a "stick to your ribs" kind of supper, but Calvin was too worried about Truman to care.

His imagination was running wild with all the horrible things that could have happened to him. Calvin couldn't keep himself from thinking the worst. Truman may have come in contact with the sheriff and his boys. That would not have ended well.

Calvin was confident Truman would have already returned under normal circumstances. He had the dreadful feeling that something had to have happened to prevent him from returning.

He prepared the palmetto, merely going through the motions, trying not to dwell on Truman's whereabouts and pretending everything was fine. After eating all the boiled palmetto he could force down, he gave Penny the rest. Calvin couldn't believe it! She didn't seem to be impressed with the stems but preferred the berries.

CHAPTER 13

The Prodigal

As usual, Calvin woke to hunger pains. No matter what, today, he had to get some fish traps in the water without being seen. The bad weather may have forced the sheriff to delay his return trip, so he had to be careful. He didn't want to be caught in the river putting out traps. Calvin also planned to set a few snares. He had seen several swamp rabbits on his last outing.

It looked like the cloud cover might break up. With the sun coming out and the wind blowing, things should start to dry. Calvin had coals from yesterday's fire, but nothing to cook. He was hungry, aggravated, and worried about Truman.

He threw a log on the coals, took the two fish traps, and made his way to the riverbank. He was determined to get the traps set, one way or the other. Once they were in the water, chances were good he would have something to eat by the afternoon.

Calvin approached the river carefully, listening for an outboard motor. All was quiet. He undressed and eased into the water up to his chest. The river was up because of the rain, but wasn't out of its banks. Still it was difficult to get in and out of the water. He managed to get only a few feet away from the bank.

He lowered this body into the muddy river and felt his way around with his hands and feet. There were exposed roots washed out from the bank. Calvin placed the traps on the bottom and tied their attached ropes to the roots just under the water so they wouldn't be seen. He pulled himself out, holding to the tree roots protruding from the bank.

He broke a cypress limb to mark the place where the traps were set. Even though it had warmed up, the water was still cool. With teeth chattering, he quickly dressed.

Calvin had a most unexpected surprise; the trip back to the cart turned out to be a trip to the meat market. After all the rain, the swamp floor was still wet and muddy. Calvin noticed an unusual trail. He wasn't sure what made it but had a pretty good idea. He decided to follow it, hoping to catch up with something for the boiling pot.

Sure enough, all the rain caused a large snapping turtle to decide to take a stroll through the swamp, perhaps looking for a new slough to hang out in.

Mr. Poole told Calvin that snapping turtles are supposed to taste like seven different types of meat. He wasn't sure, but he thought they were beef, pork, mutton, goat, shrimp, fish, and chicken. All of these would be fine at this point. He hadn't personally had the pleasure of eating turtle but couldn't wait to give it a try.

This thing looked like it weighed forty pounds. He was starving, so his survival instincts kicked in. As soon as the prehistoric crustacean saw the boy, he was instantly irritated. He threw his head back, opened his beak-like mouth, exposing its puffy white cavity with the little decoy wormlike tongue he used to fool his prey.

Calvin had heard the old wives' tale, "If a snapping turtle bites you, he will hold you until it thunders." This was one theory he didn't want to test.

He stuck a stick at his open mouth, and the turtle slammed shut with a loud clap. Calvin grabbed his tail at the same time and, with considerable trepidation, took his skinning knife and inserted it at the base of his skull. This instantly severed the spinal cord. There was no suffering. He was so grateful for this food. Like the people who lived in this swamp before him, he thanked the animal for its sacrifice.

The turtle was so heavy he could only carry it a short distance before his arm began aching. He noticed the swelling of his forearm. Its veins were visible for the first time. This was exciting for an eleven-year-old. Calvin was stumbling along, because he couldn't keep from admiring his arm. Roughing it in the swamp had developed muscles he didn't know he had. With dogged determination, he kept going, refusing to give into the pain. Finally, when he could stand it no longer, he dropped it.

He tried dragging it, but because he had to bend over so much, his back ached. His hand was sweaty and kept slipping off the tapered tail, making it difficult to keep a good grip. What would his forefathers do? He thought for a moment, then cut a slit in his tail, stuck a pole through it, and hoisted it over his shoulder.

"Much better," he said to himself.

Penny dropped from her perch as he arrived back at the makeshift camp and greeted him. Calvin approached it with caution, hoping the big dog was back and there were no unwanted guests like the sheriff and his boys.

Calvin frantically searched the place over. Maybe just maybe, Truman had returned and was waiting for him. He was kidding himself. By now he knew something had surely happened. There was nothing that would keep his dog from coming to him if he could.

Calvin realized he was going to have to get himself together soon and make some hard decisions. This wasn't a good place for a permanent camp. There was no easy source for water. When the rainwater he collected ran out, he would be forced to carry water from the river. The best thing to do now was to try and put it out of his mind and not think so much.

Calvin methodically began to prepare the turtle. He separated the top of his shell from the bottom, carefully cutting all the meat from the inside. There were subtle differences in the color and texture. He was surprised how much meat there was.

The pot was about half full of water, with some wild onions and a spoon full of salt and pepper. Once the water was boiling, he added the turtle meat. It smelled so good he was afraid every carnivore in the swamp would try to join him for supper.

This was the first real meal he had eaten in two days. As for as the different-tasting meats, he couldn't say for sure. He had never eaten mutton or goat and very little beef. Chicken, pork, wild game, and fish were the meats he was most familiar with. The only thing he knew for sure was that it was very, very good!

He ate until he couldn't eat anymore, and there was still at least ten pounds leftover. He placed a nice pile of scraps on the ground for Penny. He took the rest from the pot, wrapped them in large leaves, and placed them in the syrup bucket. Calvin poked small holes in the lid to keep blow flies off the meat. It should last for several days.

After supper, he finally made the most difficult decision since entering the swamp. He would leave in the morning, spend his last night in his little cart, and carry as much gear as possible on the slide. Then he would hide the cart by covering it with limbs and moss. His plan was to come back for it after Truman returned.

He would never give up hope, but there was no choice. He had to move on. There was little game and no water other than the river. He cut two long poles, tied them together at the small end, and strapped on only what he absolutely had to have. He would sleep in the cart tonight and, in the morning, put everything back that he couldn't take with him.

The campfire was getting low, and Calvin's spirits were even lower. The thought of moving on without Truman was almost more than he could bear. It was getting late, and knowing he had a hard day ahead, he decided to turn in early. Penny had already found a perch and began to preen herself, settling down for the night even though the sun hadn't completely set.

Calvin wasn't asleep but in deep thought when all of a sudden Penny began to cackle wildly. She then sailed from her perch toward the edge of the clearing, hitting the ground. Penny didn't miss a stride as she ran and flew at the same time toward the Prodigal, sitting on his haunches near the edge of the woods.

Calvin couldn't believe his eyes and sprinted after her shouting their welcome-home greeting as they ran.

When he was only a few feet away, Calvin's breath left him. He stopped short and dropped to his knees, franticly scanning the woods in all directions. Truman just sat there and didn't move. It was as if he was in a trance. Calvin was in disbelief; his dog had a braided lanyard around his neck.

Calvin was dizzy with emotion. Where in the world had he been all this time? Why was he wearing this perfectly platted four-strand lanyard made from palmetto palm? He took it from his neck and examined it closely. Someone had cut strands of palmetto about a quarter inch wide, skillfully plated it, and put the necklace around Truman's neck.

Calvin felt as though he was being watched and continued to visibly search the woods in all directions.

"Is anybody there?" he shouted.

All was quiet. Truman seemed to be under some kind of spell. He acted as though he didn't even recognize Calvin. This was breaking his heart!

"Hey, boy, it's me!" cried Calvin. "Don't yuh even know me?" He grabbed and hugged the big dog.

Suddenly, as if someone snapped their fingers, Truman came to. The trance had been broken. He lunged at Calvin and bowled him over backward. Calvin sprang to his feet, and the love fest began. Penny joined in the best she could.

They wrestled around on the ground. Calvin grabbed him around the neck, digging his heels in the ground trying to bulldog him like a yearling. It was too rough for Penny. Truman stepped on her foot. She let out a squawk and hobbled off with her feathers all ruffled. The two tussled until they were exhausted and collapsed in a heap.

Truman sprawled out on the ground, breathing heavily, and Calvin lay on his back with his head on the dog's belly. His head moved up and down with each breath. As Calvin causally rubbed him, he felt several bumps that had scabbed over. With closer inspection, he realized the bumps could have been inflicted from buckshot. Even though they were now scabbed over, there was one clear hole through his left ear.

Calvin knew he would probably never know how the lanyard came to be around his neck or what caused the injuries. It will always be a mystery. He wished the dog could miraculously speak to him and tell him all about it; otherwise, he would be left to wonder forever. He was so grateful that he had him back, even though he wasn't a hundred percent.

Calvin decided to stay for several more days. He didn't think the dog should be pulling the cart for a while. This would allow Truman time to completely heal.

They went back to camp, sat by a small fire, ate more turtle, and watched the sun set. Truman lay down between him and the fire. Calvin noticed when he would perk his ears up, he could see the red from the fire, through a small round hole in his left ear.

Three days had passed, and they were all together again. Truman was pulling the cart with ease and seemed to be back to his old self. They were all in good spirits. It was good to leave the old site and hopefully find a better place to camp; one with a spring would be nice.

Penny had assumed her position on top of Truman's back. She fluttered all over him, picking at the wounds for any loose scabs. It was her way of contributing to the complete recovery of her host.

Calvin's heart was overflowing as the three started a new day and a new adventure. His stomach, however, was a little empty. The turtle was all gone, and the only other meat they had was a large swamp rabbit he had caught in a snare. The first stop would be to check the fish traps.

He was surprised at how quickly the river had gone down. The tops of both traps were exposed, and now that the water level had dropped, he realized he had not put them in a very good place.

Calvin dug his toes in the black slippery mud and, with a handful of cypress branches in one hand, was able to lean forward just enough to reach the heavy cord tied to a root. He slowly pulled the traps away from the roots and onto the bank. They were both empty.

"Well, guys, guess we'll have ta do without uh little longer."

Calvin, somewhat dejected, flattened the traps, and tied them on top of the cart. The troop moved on. Even though Calvin's stomach was empty, his heart was full, and he made cheery small talk, trying to keep spirits up.

The sun was now vertical, and sweat was streaming down the back of his neck. It was getting more difficult to think of anything but food.

Truman stopped under a young leafy sweet gum tree, which provides a cool, dark, fragrant shade.

"Good idea, boy. I was thinking thu same thing," said Calvin.

They would find food; they always did. But he was still a little shaken from the empty fish traps. He just knew there would be something in them. Calvin blamed himself for setting them too close to the bank.

Penny hopped down from the giant dog's back and started scratching in the leaves.

Calvin unhooked Truman. Any other time he would let him take off and hunt for rabbits on his own, but it was too soon after his return to let him out of his sight. He sat on the ground, leaning against a tree. Truman lay beside him.

"Must be nice ta be uh chicken, huh, boy? She always finds something hidden underneath them leaves. Maybe just worms an' grubs, but she seems ta enjoy them," said Calvin.

He was plenty hungry but wasn't ready to join her just yet. He knew there may come a time. He had to choose between eating bugs and grubs or starve, but not today. Mr. Poole insisted on him trying a few fried grasshoppers, but he failed to make him like them. That will be the last resort, thought Calvin.

He felt bad that he hadn't been a better provider for all of them, but the day wasn't over. The creek was looking better for fishing. He knew his chances of catching fish later in the afternoon would be good. He had a couple of Penny's little brown eggs in the cart, and she might lay another this evening. Calvin had come to accept living with a little hunger pain; it was part of surviving off the land.

They made their way south along the riverbank to see what the day would bring. The pace was slow, for there was no reason to get in a hurry.

He needed to find a fishing pole. He always left them behind when traveling because they were too awkward to carry on the cart. There had always been a cane break every hundred yards or so, but not today.

Whenever Calvin was looking for switch cane, his thoughts would return to Mr. Poole and his favorite president, Teddy Roosevelt. He recalled the hunt of 1907 in this very swamp. After the unsuccessful bear hunt in Mississippi in 1902, President Roosevelt returned five years later to hunt bear.

He was invited by several prominent residents from Tallulah to come for a fair chase hunt in the Tensas River Bottom. The president would be guided by a couple of well-known bear hunters, along with Mr. Poole's great-grandfather, who was also an authority on the Tensas.

Mr. Poole recounted how the hunting party, with the president on horseback, ran a big black bear into a cane break. "Rowdy," Teddy's favorite hound, led the charge into the thick cane cornering the animal.

The president dismounted and went in after him. It was said he got within thirty feet of the big bruin. When the bear charged Rowdy, the president squeezed off a lethal shot, bringing the ferocious critter down.

Calvin thought how brave the president was but then surmised he was protecting his dog. What else would he do? He further pondered that and other things as they walked along searching for a patch of cane.

Calvin thought, *I have a great dog, and I named him after a president. A great president has a favorite dog, and he names him Rowdy. Who's Rowdy? Don't figure.*

Calvin checked the sun and assumed it to be about four o'clock. Fish usually bite better early morning or late afternoon, so from now until dark would be prime time. Finally, he spotted a small patch of cane with a little hole of water in the middle of it.

"This will be uh good place ta camp," he said out loud.

Truman stopped immediately as though he understood every word. After being released from the cart, the big dog began to nose around the new site.

Calvin was busy getting things ready to camp and preparing for fishing but kept an eye on Truman, at the same time. He made sure he kept him in sight for a while.

From the corner of his eye, he noticed that the dog was trotting toward the cane patch with the hair raised on his back. Truman stopped at the edge of the break and stood motionless as though pointing to the little pond.

Calvin understood he was trying to show him something. He crouched low to the ground and came up behind Truman. At first he saw nothing. Then, as he began to focus, what looked to be just part of a log became the snout and bulging eyes of an alligator.

"Yeah, I see 'im, boy. Best we leave 'im be. Come on, let's cut some cane poles an' see if we can catch some fish for supper," whispered Calvin.

The dog didn't budge but just stood there. Calvin dropped down on one knee and put an arm around the dog. He squinted his eyes while rubbing his chin, trying to size up his options. He could cut cane poles, look for bait, and then fish until dark. After they were cleaned, hopefully, there would be enough for the three of them. Or he could catch that big gator and have food for a week or more.

Calvin was hungry, and as any motivated predator, he was willing to assume risk for reward.

"Yuh know, boy, maybe yuh right," he whispered. "Thu tail on that thing has to be five feet long. Gator tail is mighty good eatin'," he thought out loud.

Calvin began to contemplate the situation. The little body of water was barely large enough for the alligator to stretch out in. Thick cane surrounded it with the exception of a crawl space under the cane, just wide enough for him to scoot back and forth to the river.

"Come on, boy, I got uh plan." They hurried back to the cart. Calvin retrieved the long plow line and the double-bit ax. He then quietly returned to the hole where the gator would crawl back and forth to the river. He made a loop with his rope around the opening of the escape tunnel through the thick cane and then tied the other end to a tree. Once the alligator's head went through the loop, the more he pulled against it, the more it would tighten. The trick was to get the loop perfectly arranged over the opening before the gator realized what was going on.

Calvin made Truman sit and wait for his signal. He quietly set the large snare. His heart was pounding as he gave a sharp whistle and then ran to the tree where the rope was tied.

Truman circled around to the back side of the little pond and began chewing and breaking the hollow bamboo. It was popping and snapping. It sounded something like a bull ramming headfirst into the thicket.

The big alligator rose up on all fours. Calvin was amazed how shallow the water was. He had wallowed out a hole just to lie in. The large reptile, aware of the intruders, had become nervous. Truman was barking, shaking cane, and making as much noise as possible. The big gator could take it no more and shot through the gap.

Calvin quickly jumped behind the tree where the rope was tied, thinking he would be safe from harm. Unfortunately, when the snare tightened around the big reptile's neck, it jerked him toward the tree that Calvin was standing behind. Then, of all things, he just kept running and rolling in circles. Before the boy had a chance to escape, he was pinned at the knees by the rope to the tree. The more frantic and angry the gator became, the harder he pulled. Each time he made a circle around the tree, the closer he came to the boy.

Calvin still had the ax but actually didn't know what to do with it. He thought about taking a swing at the rope to set the beast free, but if he missed, he might cut himself, or it would cause him to lose his grip on the ax. If he lost the ax, he would be at the mercy of a huge and very angry alligator.

Suddenly, Truman ran to his side and had to jump to avoid the rope each time it made another wrap around the tree. Calvin tried in vain to make his dog leave and get out of danger but to no avail. He would not leave. Calvin could sense Truman wasn't sure what his next move would be. But no matter what, he was going to try to protect him.

The alligator was now only a few feet away and beginning to get tired. He suddenly made eye contact with Calvin and stopped. Now there was an adversary. The reason he was tethered, the reason for his torment, and now a target for his rage.

Calvin knew this was the moment of truth. He knew Truman would die trying to save him, as he had almost done before. He was not going to let this happen. Before he had time to react, Truman jumped at the large reptile and retracted just as quickly, feeling the breeze from its jaws as they slammed shut.

Calvin's reflexes were in one motion. He leaned to one side so his backswing wouldn't hit the tree behind him. He aimed the double-bit ax at the kill spot, an inch or two behind the center of his eyes. The ax landed with a thud.

The large beast jerked backward and immediately began the death roll. The rope was cutting into Calvin's legs, and the pain was excruciating, but as luck would have it, he began turning in the opposite direction. Truman began to bark and grab at his tail while Calvin was in the process of trying to loosen the rope in order to free himself.

The dying gator's strength was leaving him. As the tension lessened, it created just enough slack for Calvin to wiggle one leg free and finally the other. He tried to run, but because the circulation had been cut off, he couldn't feel his feet. He was only able to stumble forward a little before crawling a safe distance from the gator.

Even though Calvin had dealt him a lethal blow, the gator was still twisting and rolling. In the death throw, the long tail pounded the ground uncontrollably; the long snout, with rows of teeth, was slamming shut on anything it came in contact with.

Calvin and Truman both were content just to stay out of his way. They were mesmerized by this reptile and simply watched until he slowly became still.

Calvin wasn't sure how to feel about this bizarre event, what he had witnessed, and what he had done. For some reason, of all the animals he had to kill in order for them to survive, he felt bad for this one. They both simply sat quietly, looking at the prehistoric animal long after there was no movement. He was thankful for the food, as he was for all the other animals he had killed, but the alligator had not been a threat to him or Truman. He could have gone fishing instead.

From a nearby tree, a small chicken flew down, strolled up to the ten-foot alligator, and, with great fanfare, proceeded to peck it on the tip of its tail. The gator's reflexes caused it to move a little. Penny jumped about three feet in the air, flapping her wings frantically. She was probably thinking this display of bravery might have been a big mistake if he wasn't dead.

Calvin had to laugh out loud. "Yuh better watch out, yuh silly little bird. He'll eat yuh in one bite," he said.

Penny, somewhat crestfallen, decided to disappear from sight for a while.

The laugh was a good release for Calvin. It wasn't easy taking this life, but they needed food. If he prepared it properly, it would last for weeks.

He and Truman continued to sit a while longer. They both were completely exhausted and didn't want to move.

The lack of food was taking its toll. Calvin felt faint. For the first time since he left home, he could feel his ribs and knew he had lost weight. His insect bitten arms and legs seemed smaller. The last time he had a decent meal was a few days ago. He wasn't sure he had enough energy to skin and cut up the big alligator.

Calvin remembered the three small eggs he had saved and managed to get to his feet. Still feeling light-headed, he made it back to the cart.

He retrieved the eggs, tilted his head back, and then one at a time cracked them in his open mouth. They slid all the way down to the bottom of his empty stomach. It felt like manna from heaven.

He had saved them for a whole week, not really knowing why. He usually ate the egg as soon as Penny laid one. Other times, he would save them for a special occasion; today was it. They provided just enough protein to allow him to start the cleaning process.

After the alligator was gutted, he cut Truman about three pounds of fresh meat, which he devoured with only a few gulps. He made a fire and placed a few thin stripes of the meat in the frying pan for himself.

Over the next few days, Calvin was able to set up a nice camp. By digging a deep hole in a nearby sandbar, he was able to dip out buckets of clear drinking water.

He made a smoker for the meat from the small canvas by building a tepee-like construction. From the fire pit, he dug a trench to the center of the tepee. He covered the ditch with a layer of sticks and then packed dirt on top to provide a tunnel to pull the smoke inside.

They would eat as much of the fresh meat as they could before it spoiled and smoke the rest. He also salted and dried some in the hot sun for jerky. Calvin knew he would have to spend several days getting that much meat into strips and hung inside the tent. However, after the meat was salted and smoked, it would last for weeks. With this much meat on hand, he would be free to look for a number of other plants that would provide a more balanced diet.

The plan was to stay at their new location as long as the meat lasted, and hunting and fishing were good. Calvin was determined to gain his weight back and stay healthy, not only for him but for his companions' sake.

Chapter 14

Unfinished Dream

Long after all the smoked gator was consumed, the three enjoyed their camp. Fishing had been extremely good, as well as small game hunting with his bow. Most nuts and berries were now out of season; but there were still a lot of plants, such as water crest, cattail roots, palmetto roots, wild onions, and the hips from ferns. These all made for good roughage. Gathering a variety of edible plants was time-consuming, but he knew he needed to do it.

Calvin could see and feel the results; it was amazing. His body filled out, and he no longer could see his ribs. He could feel himself growing again.

He hadn't been able to wear his shoes for quite some time. Since he started going barefooted, his toes were spreading out, and his feet seemed to be growing at an alarming rate. With no shoes, the soles of his feet had become as tough as rhino skin. He could run like a young buck deer.

He and Truman loved to race wildly through the swamp. He was convinced that under the right conditions, he might even be able to catch a rabbit with his bare hands. That never happened of course, but it was a nice fantasy.

With an ample food supply and good water, he allowed himself the luxury of being a little lazy for the first time.

Calvin thought it must be the end of July or early August. The days were long and hot. Mosquitoes, flies, and other insects were a constant irritant; but they learned to deal with it the best they could.

If the mosquitoes were too bad, he would go to the river and cover any exposed skin, especially his face, with black mud. Once it dried, there was nothing but two blue eyes peering through a mask of gray scaly delta mud. It wasn't pretty, but it sure was effective.

Neither Truman nor Penny were concerned that much. Penny welcomed any attention from insects. They were like little flying hors d'oeuvres. She was on a constant lookout for big horseflies; the loud buzzing of their wings were a dead giveaway.

They were about the only thing in the swamp that would terrify Truman. His ears would perk up as soon as he heard one, and the flight impulse would take over. It was entertaining for Calvin to watch this big brave dog fall apart when a large black horsefly would try to land on him for a sip of his blood. He was determined it wasn't going to happen, and the race was on.

Penny would join the fray, hoping to have the big bug for a juicy snack. Calvin just sat back and enjoyed the show. Penny used all the skills she possessed by running with head down and hopping high in the air all the while rapidly flapping her wings backward. This gave her amazing hang time and flight. Truman, on the other hand, could only run for his life.

Since food was a little easier to obtain, they spent a lot of time in the heat of the day trying to stay cool. In the afternoons, they would hang out in the river setting their fish traps, fishing from the bank with a cane pole, and enjoying life in the Tensas River Bottom.

Calvin began sleeping in the cart again because of the mosquito problem. On occasion, Penny would try to roost inside the cart with him, but he wasn't sure why. He thought something must have spooked her. This night, Penny was roosting in a nearby tree. Calvin was pretty sure he would have the cart to himself.

Penny would always find a roost with a maximum view to watch for Truman if he wasn't in camp when she thought he should be. This gave Calvin a heads-up when he returned.

Truman was in one of his prowling moods and hadn't returned when Calvin closed the back flaps of the cart. He sealed the cart the best he could, trying to prevent mosquitoes from entering. He had just drifted off to sleep when he heard scratching on the back of the cart. Thinking it was Penny, he kicked at the canvas flap with a bare foot.

"Shoo, get away, yuh bad chicken! Yuh woke me up," scolded Calvin! He kicked again and felt something big on the other side. Thinking it was Truman, he whispered, "Is that yuh, boy?"

The night fell silent until Penny began squawking from her roost in a way that was different than ever before.

There was a musky odor in the air and a deep guttural grunting near Calvin's ear. A crashing blow splintered one of the staves. The cart rocked to one side, almost tilting over. Then came another powerful blow, ripping a hole through the canvas. The terrified boy, lying flat on his back, was looking eye to eye with a big black bear.

The bear thrust its snarling head inside the cart. Calvin could smell his putrid breath from his gaping mouth as it let out a thundering growl. Drool fell on Calvin's face as he covered his head with his hands. The bear had no idea what was inside the cart. In most cases, a black bear would run from a human. This wasn't most cases. He was a big hungry male, and Calvin smelled like food.

The bear started pushing on the cart with short powerful thrusts from his huge forearms. The cart began rolling downhill. All Calvin could do was lay there hoping Truman would come back.

Calvin remembered the leftover fish in the syrup bucket hanging on the side of the cart. Maybe that's what the bear wanted and not him.

He managed to reach under the side of the canvas and untie the string with one hand the bucket fell off. The cart rolled a few more yards and rammed into a tree.

The big bear saw the bucket fall and stopped. He was busy tearing the lid off as Calvin jumped through the hole in the canvas and ran for his life. The bear was startled to see Calvin leap from the cart and ran off in the other direction.

Calvin was a little put out with Truman when he came strolling back to camp the next morning. He spent the next day replacing the stave and sewing up the hole.

The days were slipping by quickly for the boy and his dog. Summer would soon be gone. There were still a few wild grapes and muscadine. The locals called them possum grapes. Both fruits were sweet, and both had tough skins and big seeds, but Calvin loved them anyway.

Calvin would gather as many as possible and eat them for snacks. He also would put some in his skillet, cook them down, and spoon the sweet nectar over fried fish or anything else for that matter.

Possums and raccoons would be trying to harvest the same fruit. If he was lucky, he might have wild game with a fruit marmalade. Penny spent a considerable amount of time among the vines of wild grapes and muscadine, but as with all seasons, summer was coming to an end.

There was for the first time a change in the air. It was welcomed but brought with it a touch of sadness. He didn't understand why, but he began missing Emily Mae even more. The change in the air brought with it a sense of guilt. It wouldn't be long before kids were back in school. He certainly didn't miss that, but somewhere down deep, he knew that when he became an adult, he would regret not having finished all twelve grades.

The cooler days also brought thoughts of surviving winter in the bottom. He was sure the struggles they would face would be compounded with cold weather. Thoughts of the cold early spring, waking up soaked to the bone and shivering, would probably be nothing compared to what lay ahead. There would come a time when the temperature would drop to the low twenties, and ice would form on the whole swamp.

Calvin decided to put those thoughts aside, he would deal with winter when it arrived. In the meantime enjoy the break from the heat and humidity.

Their camp had provided all the necessities for survival, but that never seemed to be enough for Calvin. His youthful desire for adventure, and the first signs of autumn made him decide it was time to move on.

The three nomads had wandered a mile or so away from the river, because the trail following the bank had large ditches that were washed out by early spring rains. It was much easier for Truman to pull the cart on level terrain. He figured they could always work their way back toward the river to make camp.

"This looks pretty good. We'll stop for the night."

Truman took full advantage of being unhitched from the cart and bounded off with his big nose to the ground.

Calvin glanced in his direction and shouted, "You be careful out there! Don't let a bugger get ya." He then went about his evening chores of gathering firewood.

He was in the process of digging a shallow hole for the fire. At the same time, he used the opportunity to bust open the clods for Penny, exposing a few night crawlers for her supper. Then he heard a familiar sound.

Truman always made an introductory bark of sorts that was different from all other barks he made. It was like he was clearing his throat before giving a speech to a large crowd to get their attention.

Over the past months, the two had become as one. When it came to hunting, each anticipated what the other needed in order to complete the task.

Calvin stopped what he was doing and listened closely in order to pinpoint the direction. He knew Truman was about to mark the tree the varmint went up. There was always a little hesitation between the introductory bark and the tree bark. It was the length of time it took for him to make absolutely sure the squirrel was in the tree. Sometimes, they would only run up a tree for a few feet and then jump onto another, scamper down to the ground, and run up another many yards away trying to trip up the dog.

Dogs of lesser ability were prone to give up and just start barking up the wrong tree, so to speak. This would gain them the reputation of being a "lying dog," and to the hunter there is nothing worse. This was not the case with Truman! He would make ever-widening circles around the tree with his nose to the ground to make sure that didn't happen. He would rather never tree again than make a mistake.

Calvin continued to listen for the tree bark, but it seemed the big dog was having a little trouble marking the tree. It was taking longer than usual.

Calvin cupped both hands around his mouth and shouted, "Hunt 'em up, boy. Speak to 'em."

This was his special way of encouragement. It also let Truman know that he had heard him and was waiting for him to tree.

Finally, Truman let out the tree bark. With that, Calvin grabbed his bow and ran toward the barking. He was hoping for a little red meat for the frying pan.

He could tell from Truman's barking it was close to a half mile away, and the sun was already getting low. With little sunlight left, it would make it even more difficult to find the game. There was a sense of urgency to get there as soon as possible and perhaps add some squirrel meat with the leftover fish he had planned to eat.

He was only a few yards from Truman when he realized this was a most unusual set of circumstances. At the foot of a freestanding fireplace, Truman sat with a somewhat sheepish look on his face. He seemed a little confused and, if he could talk, would probably say, "I can't help it! That's where he is."

Everyone in this part of the country had heard the saga of the Norman Frisby plantation. Mr. Poole had mentioned it many times and told Calvin they would try to find it one day.

Calvin couldn't believe he was standing in the middle of what was to be the grandest home in the Mississippi Delta. This home, however, was never finished.

Rumor had it that Norman Frisby was killed by Orlando Flowers, his brother-in-law. It was said there was never any love lost between the two.

Mr. Frisby had grandiose ideas of building the most imposing cotton plantation in all the southland. He had put together twenty thousand acres in the Tensas River Bottom. While building this empire, he also had made several enemies and incurred an enormous debt. The Civil War was raging, and it wasn't looking good for the confederacy. Norman Frisby was like a man possessed. He was trying to finish his magnificent home for his wife and seven children hoping to ward off the Union before they took everything. A man on edge from all accounts, it didn't take much for the powder keg to explode.

The encounter took place at the river crossing in 1863. An argument between Norman Frisby and Orlando Flowers occurred when Frisby accused Flowers of stealing his mule. Some say this was just an excuse to settle an old score. Frisby attacked Flowers with his whip while they both were on horseback and knocked him to the ground. Frisby dismounted, and the two scuffled on the bank of the river until Flowers pulled out his large Bowie knife. He stabbed Frisby three times. The third struck him in the chest. The blow was lethal, but it took forty-five minutes for him to die. He called Orlando over to him and said he had rather be breathing his last breath than be in the brother-in-law's shoes. He died under the shade of an oak tree on the east bank of the Tensas.

The master of what was going to be the most magnificent plantation ever built was dead, and with his death, the unfinished plantation died with him. Two years later, the war was over, and there was little left. His widow freed the slaves and moved to Texas with her children.

Mr. Poole spoke of treasure buried somewhere on the property. It was a silver bell. Supposedly, Frisby, knowing the Union soldiers were pillaging all the plantations of their valuables, had all the silver melted down and cast into a large bell. It was rumored that he had a slave hitch a couple of mules to a wagon and carry the bell deep into the swamp. The slave was ordered to dig a deep hole to bury the bell in. Once the hole was finished, Frisby killed the slave and pushed him into the hole along with the bell, burying both together. This was disputed by the Frisby family, but it added even more intrigue to a very sad and tragic story. The bell and the slave were never seen again.

Suddenly, Truman jumped up on the side of the large fireplace after catching a glimpse of a gray squirrel shoot out the top of the chimney. In an instant, the squirrel leaped from a limb that hung just above the chimney to an adjacent tree. Without ever touching ground, it leaped from tree to tree and disappeared in the dark forest.

"That's okay, boy. We still have some fish." Calvin sighed.

They took a little time to survey the foundation of the old plantation. It was huge. Several fireplaces and a few walls with cornerstones still stood, but now large trees were standing where the great rooms would have been.

Calvin tried to imagine what it would be like to live in such a place. The idea of having other people wait on you hand and foot was so foreign to anything he would want. It was impossible for him to relate to. There was something disturbing about this place. It was as though it should have never been here in the first place and the swamp was slowly reclaiming its own.

"Come on, boy," whispered Calvin. "Lets' get out uh here. This place gives me the creeps."

The morning passed slowly on empty stomachs. They ate all the leftover fish last night. Calvin was hoping they might luck up and find something before they stopped for the night.

Truman stopped and perked his ears up. Calvin knew he had heard something, but he hadn't heard what the dog was hearing. They all stood still and listened. Even Penny, who had been walking beside the cart stopped scratching in the leaves, raised her head, then cocked it to one side in order to hear better.

Finally, he heard a soft buzzing sound. "That's it!" shouted Calvin and pointed to a swarm of bees high over their heads. The old hollow tree leaned to one side. There was a large split at the bottom wide enough for Calvin to stick his head in and, with a little effort, his whole body.

"Come here, Truman! Look at this! Bet this ol' thing is full of honey!"

The thought of wild honey impaired his ability to consider the risks involved in trying to obtain it. Calvin stood there for a while just gazing up at the knothole.

There was a cloud of bees guarding the entrance. The knothole was about ten feet from the ground. From inside the hollow, he could see light shining through the knothole. With their heads stuck inside the hollow trunk, he and the dog studied the situation.

"Man, I sure wish I had some of that bee honey! How 'bout yuh, buddy boy?" asked Calvin. "I can see thu honeycombs now that my eyes are used to thu dark. I think we can reach it with uh pole an' pull it down. I'll make uh hook out of uh forked stick an' tie it on thu end of thu pole. What do yuh think?" he asked Truman.

The big dog seemed to be in agreement, and Penny was too busy scratching up lunch to be concerned.

After securing a pole long enough to reach the honeycombs, he tied a forked stick to the pole, with the forks facing down.

"Okay, now we need ta make sure we don't get stung by uh hundred bees," said an apprehensive Calvin.

He cut two eyeholes in his burlap sack. The plan was to slip it over his head at the point of attack. He covered Truman with moss, securing it with small flexible vines, hoping these two precautions would keep him from being stung.

They began making their way back to the old bee tree. Calvin laughed out loud when Truman trotted in front of him. He had tied moss around Truman's neck and around his middle. Moss was dragging on the ground from his waist, making him walk funny in order not to step on it.

Calvin put the sack over his head and arranged the eyeholes so he could see. Carefully crawling inside the hollow tree, he waited long enough for his eyes to adjust and then lifted the hook above the cones.

The hook was a little hard to control. The tip of the pole was flimsy, which allowed it to swivel back and forth. He bumped them several times, and each time the bees would flare up. They were stinging the stick and dive-bombing in all directions. They were already enraged by the time he felt the hook snag the cones.

Calvin was trying to push the big dog back out of the way, so he would have a clear path to run. Truman banged into him, causing the hook to dislodge a large slab of honeycomb. The bee-infested slab came crashing down.

Calvin tried to back out the way he came in, but Truman was blocking the exit. His eyeholes had turned ninety degrees, making him blind as a bat. Stomping around inside the hollow, he felt warm sticky nectar between his toes, along with a hundred sharp pin-like sensations. The bees were now underneath the sack.

Once again, it was every man for himself. At last, Calvin was able to propel himself from the hollow tree; and both, he and Truman, ran for their lives. Truman's armor of moss had proven itself to be worthless, as had Calvin's "sack over the head" apparatus. Both had their sight impaired, and the extra weight just slowed them down.

They were running wildly through the woods. Calvin managed to push one eyehole over enough to glimpse the ground. Still he ran into trees and tripped over limbs. Truman's moss had slipped all the way back to his hind legs and looked a little like a grass skirt, flowing in the breeze. Both were pursued by a little stream of tormentors, which occasionally would connect enough to produce a flailing of arms, or, in Truman's case, a spinning around and nipping at the rear end.

Calvin didn't look down quickly enough to avoid a root. A bare foot caught it, and he sailed headfirst, hitting something big. The large object gave way with a swooshing sound, when the boy's head hit it dead center. He landed on top of the large object. For a moment, it was motionless; then he felt it begin to shake and make deep bellowing sounds. These sounds reached high-pitched squeals, which faded into silence. The same sequence repeated over and over again.

Calvin was thoroughly confused. His head was spinning, and the back of his neck was hurting. He threw off the sack, which still held trapped angry bees.

He had just knocked the breath out of a heavy, tall elderly black man. He rolled off and sat up, rubbing the back of his neck.

"You must be Preacher Joe. I heard some men talking 'bout you," said Calvin.

CHAPTER 15

Preacher Joe

The old man was trying to catch his breath but couldn't while shaking with laughter. Tears had formed in the corners of his eyes. Each time he tried to speak, uncontrollable laughter erupted all over again.

Calvin just sat there beside him. He didn't know what hurt the most, the hundred beestings or the back of his neck.

Suddenly, the old man stopped laughing and slapped his forehead.

"I lost my glasses. Yuh must uf knocked dem off when yuh head butted me in thu belly. Hold on now. Don't nobody move. Dey gotta be right here somewheres," he said.

Calvin caught a glimpse of the sun's reflection through one of the lenses. The glasses were only a foot or two from where he was sitting. He picked them up and handed them to the preacher. With glasses in hand, he resumed his laughter.

By this time, Calvin was a little embarrassed and somewhat put out. He had a hundred beestings, his neck was hurting, and he had been accused of knocking the old man's breath out and losing his glasses. The old fella was still laughing so hard he could barely speak. Calvin, for life of him, didn't see what was so funny.

There wasn't a word between them for what seemed to Calvin, an uncomfortable duration. The old man was consumed in his thoughts, smiling and mumbling to himself.

All of a sudden, Truman bounded out of nowhere, spinning around right between them, nipping at beestings on his rear end. It wasn't until he saw the honey between Calvin's toes and began licking it that he forgot about the stings.

The old preacher snapped out of his daze and began thunderous laughter again. "Dat sho is some kin'da dog! I've plowed mules no bigger dan 'im," said the preacher.

Calvin was relieved the old man was back. The silence was uncomfortable for him.

"My name is Calvin Young," he said, trying to engage the old man in conversation.

About that time, there was quite a bit of noise created by, what seemed to Calvin, an exaggerated flapping of wings as Miss Penny made her appearance. She always did that when she wanted attention.

The old preacher shouted, "Whar dat chicken come from? Dat's my li'l ol' bannie hen. Some uf dem moonshiner boys stole 'bout half dozen uf my laying hens. Dey got dat li'l ol' bannie, but I don't care 'bout it, 'cause her eggs wuz too little," said the preacher. "Not worth thu feed."

"She just showed up one day. I didn't steal her or nothing, but thu little eggs sure are good, though," said Calvin. Calvin wasn't sure he should admit he knew all about the two moonshiners.

The old man didn't seem to hear Calvin when he introduced himself, so Calvin decided to do it again.

"My name is Calvin Young," a little louder this time.

For the first time, he turned and looked at Calvin and with a big smile and said, "I knows who yuh is. I knowed yo' momma an' daddy. I knowed uf yo' grandpappy but never did see 'im. He wuz uh Indian," said the preacher. Calvin was somewhat taken back by this revelation.

"Now tell me, boy. What yuh doing in dis ol' swamp all by yoself?" asked Preacher Joe.

Calvin hesitated. He wasn't sure if he should tell his life's story at this point.

"Well, dat's all right. Let's go git dat honey. Den we'll talk. What yuh say 'bout dat? Get yuh sack yuh throwed away. We'll put thu honey cones in it."

"Yes, sir," said an excited Calvin.

When the old man stood, Calvin was surprised at how straight and tall he was. Most people his age were a little bent over. This man was the oldest person he had really ever talked to.

He loved the way he molded each word and dispensed them through his thick lips, kind of like a cat purring. He spoke using the fewest words possible in order to make the point. It was something like shorthand for the spoken word. He used jesters and expressions with a voice that rumbled like some kind of musical instrument with lots of pitch and tone. It was fascinating to Calvin.

"Yeah, I done heard yo li'l ol' wagon coming thru de swamp fo two miles. All dem pots an' pans clanging together makes uh racket. So I's came out ta see who's making all dat racket, an' 'bout dat time yawl come running out uh dat ol' bee tree." His eyes were twinkling as he spoke. "Yuh boys put on quite da show. I ain't laughed dat much in uh while. Did dey sting yuh?"

He rubbed the back of his neck. "Yes sir, 'bout uh hundred times," said Calvin with a numb lip that was swelling from one of those stings.

"Yo sho is a tuff young'un . . . Yo sho is."

Calvin straightened his shoulders in reply to the great compliment he had just received.

"How old are yuh, son?" he asked.

"Eleven. How old are you?" asked Calvin.

The old preacher rubbed his chin as they walked back to the bee tree.

"Don't know fo sho. When I wuz uh young 'un, dare wuz 'bout six or eight uf us, some died as babies. Our momma wrote thu year down in thu Bible when we wuz born. But thu house burned down, an' thu ol' Bible wuz burnt up. She couldn't remember all thu years everybody wuz born. It don't matter, 'cause thu good Lord knows, an' he's de only one dat counts. But I thank 'bout eighty-five or ninety years," said Preacher Joe with a laugh.

"Dat's de biggest dawg I ever did see. How yuh come by 'im?"

"It's kind uh long story," said Calvin.

"Sho 'nuff, we'll take de honey back ta camp. I'll make some hot biscuits, an' we can talk some," said the preacher.

Calvin's eyes rolled back in his head at the thought.

The slab full of wild honey was now abandoned by the bees. It was just lying there for the taking. Calvin handed the preacher the sack and scooted inside the hollow tree to retrieve the heavy sticky slab. The preacher held the sack open as Calvin carefully placed it inside.

Calvin licked the gooey nectar between his fingers, producing a smile from ear to ear.

"Oh, that's mighty good," he said, smacking his lips.

Truman watched with saliva dripping off his tongue as Calvin licked his fingers. He was determined to get his big head inside the tree to help clean up the honey dripping off Calvin's hands.

"Get back, Truman! Let me pull thu rest down," said Calvin as he grabbed the pole still leaning on the inside wall of the hollow.

"Wait! We needs ta make uh smoke outa dem damp leaves." The preacher pointed to the ground inside the tree. "Yuh got any matches?" he asked.

"No, sir, but I've got some coals in my syrup bucket if they ain't gone out."

The preacher walked to the back of the cart where the bucket was hanging. He took it off and felt the bottom of the bucket.

"Still hot," he said as he removed the lid, blew on them until they glowed red, and handed the bucket to Calvin.

The boy dumped out a couple of bright red coals onto the damp leaves inside the tree. He covered them with more and blew until the smoke began rolling up the insides of the hollow and out the knothole.

"Dey won't bite yuh now. Grab dat pole an' pull de combs down," said the old preacher.

They filled the sack with twenty pounds of honeycombs.

The first thing Calvin noticed was a water pump that stood next to the porch. *What a luxury*, he thought. The little cabin, with real walls and a couple of windows, was filled with the aroma of biscuits rising in the muffin pan. Calvin could barely contain himself with the thought of wild honey and biscuits in his future. He could feel the saliva forming in the corners of his mouth.

Truman had been napping on the porch, but when the glorious vapors from the potbellied stove reached Truman's rather large nostrils, he sprang to his feet and stuck the big nose inside the open door. There was a wild look in his eyes, and his foot-long tongue was drooling all over the floor.

"Looks like yuh boys ready fo some hot biscuits an' honey. Got some butter too! Now dat's gone'a be larapin good," said the preacher.

There was a frenzy. Sounds of slurping, sopping, then moaning, and groaning because all three had bellies ready to pop. After the feast, sleep wasn't far away.

Calvin spread his quilt in the corner of the cabin, Truman lay on the porch, and Penny settled down in a nearby cypress tree so she could keep an eye on the big dog.

The old preacher had a cot made with ropes threaded across a wooden frame and a thin cotton mattress. For the first time in months, Calvin had another human being to carry on a conversation with. Plus, he was in a house with a tin roof. Both were luxuries. He wasn't sure he should get used to it, but for the moment it was wonderful. He could barely keep tears from forming in his eyes.

He felt guilty whenever things were this good for him. He would always think of Emily Mae, wondering if she had new parents and if she missed him as much as he missed her. The preacher was such a wonderful old man. He was thinking it probably wouldn't be a good idea to get to comfortable here. Things never seemed to last for Calvin or those he cared about.

Calvin awoke to the hollow sound created by a boat paddle clonking on the side of a waterlogged cypress boat. He sat up and stretched. He had slept until the sun was up for the first time since he arrived in the swamp.

Through the open door, he could see the sun trying to burn through the mist. The familiar smell of the river shared the first whispers of autumn. The definite change in the air was exhilarating. Calvin shivered a little as he walked out on the porch in only his long handles.

Truman had been down at the riverbank watching the preacher check a trotline. When he saw Calvin, he wheeled around and ran up the steep steps to greet him.

The camp was built on the highest point on this side of the river. It perched on fifteen-foot poles because of the possibility of flooding. But even at that height there were no guarantees.

Their greeting was as though they hadn't seen each other for months. Miss Penny, of course, got in on the act with a little cackling.

The three walked down to the riverbank to help the preacher with a fish stringer holding fifteen or twenty large channel catfish. Calvin grabbed the rope and held the boat in place as the preacher swung the heavy stringer of catfish on to the bank.

"Wow, that's a nice stringer of channel cats," said Calvin.

"Dey bring de most money, but I hav'ta run the trotline. Buffalo fish just bottom feeders won't bite no trotline. I catch dem in traps. Dey easy to catch, but only folk's dat can't afford catfish will eat buffalo fish. We'll have some of dem cats fo supper, if yuh gone 'a be around," said the old man with a smile.

Calvin just smiled a little and nodded the affirmative.

"Good, take off three big good'uns fo us an' put de rest in thu pen." He motioned to a large square box. It had a wooden frame covered with chicken wire and tied with a rope to a cypress root on the bank.

Calvin carefully avoided the poisonous fins on the three large fish and lay them on the bank. He opened the lid and dropped the others into the box. Only the top of the box was visible above the water, but Calvin estimated the box to be about six feet square and full of catfish and buffalo fish.

"Wow, how many yuh got in here?" Calvin asked.

"Don't know fo sho, but thu fish market man be coming to pick 'um up in uh few days. He comes from Tallulah." He nodded toward the other side of the bank.

"Thu river cuts close ta de road on de other side, not more'n uh half mile. Sometime in de winter, when all de leaves off de trees, yuh can almost see cars go by."

Calvin had no idea he was that close to the outside world. He could make out the road and a small dock where the fish market man would pick up Preacher Joe's catch for the market.

"What's that rope for with that jar tied to it?" asked Calvin.

"Dat's my telegraph," he laughed. "Got pulleys on both ends, so I's can put uh little note in da jar, an' pull it ta thu yuther side. Don't read or write much, but can put down uh few words on paper. Dat uh way, thu fish market man don't have'ta cross de river, ta tell me sump 'in, if I ain't here. He's just put thu note in de jar, and pull it ta my side," said the preacher.

Calvin realized at that point that each moment at the camp with Preacher Joe was taking a great risk. Sooner or later, someone would spot him there and notify the sheriff. He wanted to stay as long as he could, because the preacher said he knew his mother and father and even knew of his grandfather. There were a lot of questions he wanted to ask the old man. Calvin liked the preacher very much, and if he asked him to stay a while, he would. But he also knew he would have to be prepared to leave when the time came.

Chapter 16

Preacher Joe Makes a Revelation

The day before the fish market man was to pick up the catch, Calvin hitched Truman to the cart, and they went deep into the woods behind the camp. They spent the night. He couldn't take a chance on being seen.

Over the next several weeks, Calvin and the preacher ran trotlines and checked the traps. In the afternoon, they sat on the porch and ate fried catfish with biscuits and honey.

One evening after supper, the preacher and his three guests were sitting on the porch, enjoying the river and the music of the swamp.

"Calvin, will yuh go ta heaven one day, when yo days end on dis earth?" asked the preacher.

Calvin was shocked by the question, right out of the blue. He found it impossible to make a coherent response. Finally, he almost shouted, "I have to! My mother's there."

The preacher nodded his approval with a big smile and said, "Well, dat's all I wants ta know. Wes's brothers den, so fer now own, yuh be Brother Calvin an' I be Brother Joe."

The preacher recounted his early life as a sharecropper and how he moved from one large cotton farm to another. He was good at it but didn't like it. He always wanted to work just for himself.

"I didn't like being 'round folks much. Den I met Eller, thu closest thang ta uh angel dat ever walked dis earth. She showed me da Lord."

He paused with his eyes closed for what seemed to Calvin to be an eternity. He just sat there mumbling to himself. Calvin wasn't sure what to do. He leaned forward in his chair to see if his eyes were still closed and was about to ask if he was okay, when the preacher opened his eyes.

"Eller says she thinks it be best fer yuh ta stay here uh spell."

Calvin breathed a heavy breath of relief. Dealing with another human being seemed far more demanding than dealing with his other companions. He realized the old man was suspended between the past and present as he moved frequently between the two. He didn't have the ability to know the difference.

"Do yuh think my daddy's dead?" asked Calvin.

"If my daddy was back, he'd come looking for me, I know he would," said Calvin.

"Yeah, I speck he would. Yo daddy an' me wuz farming cotton fer uh fella on de 'uther side uf Tallulah. Never saw nobody so proud uf his baby boy, as yuh daddy. All he wanted ta talk 'bout wuz you," said the preacher with a twinkle in his eye.

Hearing the preacher say how much his daddy loved him was a priceless gift Calvin would treasure forever.

"I likes ta speak de gospel ta 'im. He wanted ta know all 'bout it, 'cause he wuz gone 'a join de army. He wuz just uh boy, didn't want ta go, but he did what he felt he had ta. He loved his baby boy an' yo momma and wanted ta keeps yawl frum harm. Den he went off ta war. Maybe he'll come back, hopes he does. He wuz uh good boy," said the preacher.

Calvin realized his dad would have been in his early twenties. Preacher Joe was an old man. It didn't make sense that they were doing the same job.

"When yo mama died, I help dig her grave. I had seen yuh at de service, standin' with yo head down, but no crying. Yuh wuz with some folks I didn't know, and de lady wuz holding yo baby sister."

"That was thu Pooles at thu foster home," said Calvin.

He couldn't believe the connection between the old man and his father.

The preacher could tell the boys eyes were pleading for more. He tried to remember every single detail he could about the boy's father, but his memory was foggy.

"What about my grandpa that was Indian. I feel like I'm more Indian than white," said Calvin. "That's how come I'm living on thu river."

"Is dat right? I been gone 'a talk ta yuh 'bout dat. I hear folks talkin' 'bout uh wild boy living down in thu swamp. Uther folks say he drowned in thu river."

"Some folks had been talkin' 'bouts uh swamp monster an' uh big ol' dog goin' 'round biten folks. Yuh don't know nut'in 'bout dat, do yuh?" the preacher chuckled.

"I spec' yuh should be goin' back home, don't yuh, Brother Calvin?"

Calvin didn't respond for a while, then said, "I don't have uh home. It would be better for everyone if I lived in the swamp, especially my little sister."

Calvin repeated his question about his Indian grandfather. His response touched the preacher's heart, so he stopped questioning him.

"How much do yuh know 'bout yo Indian grandpappy?"

"Not much. I don't think my daddy an' momma knew much. Nobody would ever talk about him," said Calvin.

"I reckon not," said the old man. After another long pause, the preacher spoke. "I probably ort not tell yuh dis, 'cause it's just uh story. I never did lay eyes on 'im myself, but guess yuh have uh right to know what some folks say 'bout 'im."

"Folks say yo grandpappy wuz uh tall, dark, an' handsome Indian, an' he wanted ta marry dis white girl. Her daddy wuz uh big cotton farmer. Yo grandpappy had been working for 'im uh spell an' wuz smitten by his daughter."

"Thu wealthy cotton farmer didn't want his daughter ta marry up with no Indian, with thu name Young Hawk. They wuz just kids but in love an' begged thu old man ta let 'em git married. Yo grandpappy said he wud change his Indian name."

"Thu cotton farmer finally gave in, so he switched it round an' made it Hawk Young. Dat's how yuh git yo last name," said the preacher.

Calvin didn't know much about his grandfather, but he knew this and didn't dare stop him. He wanted to hear any information the old fella might know about his family.

"After dey married up, yo grandpappy raised uh crop of cotton but really wanted ta raise corn. Thu old man didn't know nut 'n 'bout no corn, but yo grandma talked him into lettin' 'im try it.

"Well, da next year, yo Indian grandpa raised thu biggest crop uf corn ever been raised in dis neck uf de woods. Folks came from all over ta talk ta yo grandpappy 'bout how he done it.

"He figured with his share uf de money, he could buy 'em uh little piece uh land. Since yo daddy wuz now 'bout uh year old, dey wanted ta own uh place uf dey own.

"Dis made thu ol' man mad, 'cause dis young Indian wuz gittin' all thu attention.

"Big landowners wanted ta talk ta 'im 'bout grow'n corn. Dey says dey would give 'im uh bigger share dan what he wuz offered from his own wife's daddy. De usual share wuz half. So after dey paid off da landowner, dey might have uh nuff to buy a little spot uf land uf der own.

"Den thu ol' man heard 'em talkin' 'bout moving off with his grandson. Dey says he loved his grandson, yo daddy, so he broke his word. He told yo grandpappy thu first year he gits all de corn. It'd be da second year befo' he'd git half.

"Everybody knowed it wuz uh lie. Yo word wuz yo bond ta uh Indian. Dis didn't set well with yo grandpappy.

"Thu way I heard it, he moved out uf thu sharecropper's shack an' left yo grandma an' daddy. He wuz Indian and didn't think like uh white man. He wuzn't use ta people breakin' they's promise. De's man broke uh promise, an' yo grandpappy wanted ta git revenge.

"He decided ta make uh trip back ta thu reservation in Texas and ta stay fo uh spell. All de folks on de reservation knowed yo grandpappy had de gift an' could walk with thu spirits. Uh lot'uh people on thu reservation wuz scared uf 'im. Dey didn't zackly welcome 'im back, but he wanted ta talk ta his daddy.

"Young Hawk had thu gift an' could cast spells on folks, either fo good or bad. One morning, he just showed back up in Louisiana.

"Thu corn wuz stored in de big barn dat had uh tin roof, with one uf dem weather vanes on top. De weather vane had uh long rod, with uh little horse standin' at de top, dat would spin around ta show which ways de wind's blowing.

"Folks say he climbed on thu roof an' tied some horse hair on de little metal horse. Den for a couple uf weeks, at straight up twelve o'clock, de Indian would just appear out uf no wheres. He'd set right in thu middle uf thu wood pile an' stare at de weather vane. Wouldn't talk ta nobody, not even yo grandma, den just disappeared again.

"One day yo grandma an' daddy wuz inside thu barn, some say gatherin' eggs, when de clock strike twelve. Yo grandpappy had no idea dey wuz inside.

"He wuz staring at dat weather vane. Den, out uf de blue sky, uh strike of lightin' come straight fum de sun an' hit dat weather vane. It knocked thu little horse off, an' de bolts broke loose. De center rod dropped thirty foot, as yo grandma bent over ta pick up eggs. It went through her back an' stuck three feet in de ground, pinning her facedown.

"De red-hot rod caught de hay on fire. De whole barn wuz on fire when yo grandpappy run in ta save 'em, but when he grabbed hold uf thu rod his hands stuck, all he could do wuz peel'em off, pick up thu baby, an' run out.

"Folks come runnin' fum all over, but it wuz too late. When thu barn start fallin' in, some folks say dey thought dey heard yo grandma screamin'. Dat whole tin roof just fell flat ta da ground. Thu only thang stickin' up wuz dat rod. It poked through thu roof, still glowin' red, sept fo thu skin uf yo grandpappy's hands. Dey's wuz burnt black, still stickin' ta dat rod.

"Folks wuz screamin' an' cryin. Den all uf uh sudden, dey turned on yo grandpappy, started yellin', an' pointin' at de Indian, 'Witchcraft! Bad medicine! Yuh done it! Yuh killed her!' dey say.

"He told 'em he didn't know dey wuz inside. But dey wouldn't hear none uf it.

"Dey say folks wuz scared uf yo grandpappy. De once handsome man now looks like uh monster. All de hair burnt off his head. He had big blisters all over an' skin drippin' off his face.

"Yo grandpappy reached in his pocket with hands dat look like nut'en but blood an' bones. He took out uh gold pocket watch with uh chain an' hung it on thu baby's neck, den handed yo daddy ta uh woman. And den he just disappeared. Nobody ever saw him again.

"Uf de folks dat wuz thar, some say he would've died fum all dem burns. Some say he went crazy in de head, 'cause he couldn't pull dat rod out uf yo grandmas back an' run off an' died in dis very swamp.

"Some say dat he's de swamp monster. Folks make out like dey see him, but I been fishin' an' huntin' in dis ol' swamp all my life, an' I ain't never seen no monster.

"Did yuh know all dat?" asked the preacher.

Calvin was stunned. His ears were ringing. It was as though the words were slammed to the side of his head and had left him semiconscious. His mouth was gaped open as he tried to speak but gave up and sat motionless instead. It was too much for his eleven-year-old brain to comprehend.

Neither spoke for a long time. Suddenly, Calvin jumped up and ran toward the cart behind the cabin.

"Where ar' yuh going, Brother Calvin!" shouted the preacher.

"I'll be right back," Calvin answered over his shoulder.

He returned and proudly held the watch by the chain for the preacher to see.

"It's my watch. I have it! My daddy gave it to my momma, and she gave it to me before she died. Look on thu back. It says, 'Hawk Young.'"

"Well, yuh don't say. It sho do."

Chapter 17

The Wooden Village

The days were indescribably beautiful. The mornings had a slight touch of autumn. The great cypress trees appeared to have had a watercolorist water down a little yellow ochre and cad Indian red and run a wash over the once bright green leaves.

Since the three travelers had become guests at the fish camp, life was so much easier. In the past, two-thirds of the day was spent searching for food.

At the cabin, they still ate mostly fish, but there was always plenty. The preacher also had potatoes, beans, fixings for biscuits, and corn bread. He still had a dozen laying hens, so they had plenty of eggs. Every time the fish market man showed up, the preacher would do some trading for staples, such as lard, baking powder, flour, and meal.

Calvin knew when the fish market man was supposed to show up. At these times, he and Truman would go on a hunting trip. They returned to the fish camp after a couple of nights alone in the swamp, bringing with them a few squirrels.

Brother Joe loved to eat fried squirrel with mashed potatoes and gravy. He had hunted them out around the camp, so Calvin knew he would be surprised with their success. It was Calvin, however, who was surprised.

Brother Joe met him on the porch, holding a big watermelon. "Guess what I got here!"

Calvin's eyes bugged at the sight.

"Well, I'll tell yuh. It's one uf dem watermelons yuh always talkin' 'bout, from over in Jackson Parish. I knowed its gitin' late in de season an' watermelons 'bout all gone, so I told thu fish market man ta find us one. Go put it in the river to git cold."

After eating squirrels and biscuits with gravy for supper, the preacher told Calvin to get the melon from the river. By now he knew it would be nice and cold. He put their prize on the porch, and they sat down on the steps, one on each side of the melon.

Calvin rubbed its cool green-striped skin. The preacher thumped it a couple of times.

"I hope it ain't too ripe." He took out his pocketknife and pushed it into the heart. With little effort, there was a pop, and the melon split open, exposing its frosty red goodness.

"Go git us some spoons." He flashed a big grin at Calvin.

"O yeah, it's gone'a be a good'un," said the old fella.

They both ate half, down to the pink rind, then gave the rest to Penny.

She perched on the outside rind and pecked it clean. Her head feathers were slicked back, soaking wet with watermelon juice. She was so full she couldn't fly to her perch, so she just squatted in the corner of the porch.

After the watermelon party, there was an absence of conversation. The musical sounds of the river made the preacher sleepy. He titled his head back, and Calvin knew what that meant. He would be sawing gourds in no time. Truman was already napping.

Calvin slipped quietly inside and pulled his project from under his pillow and started whittling away. He had been carving a little figure about six inches high out of soft dry cypress. Calvin recalled his decision to start the carving.

Only a few months before Mr. Poole passed away, he said, "Calvin, my boy, there are a few things I want you to remember: 'Don't put things off until tomorrow that you can do today,' 'You must try to learn something new every day, never lose your curiosity, and never take tomorrow for granted.' 'If we are lucky, we may make seventy or so trips around the sun on this little old planet, but that's not up to us.'"

Mr. Poole was not that lucky.

Last September, Calvin, along with most of the foster kids, had earned a little money picking cotton. They chose to spend some of it at the fall carnival.

There were several attractions that required a ticket: a five-hundred-pound fat lady, a woman with a beard, a skinny sword swallower, and a strong man with a lot of tattoos who could lift a three-hundred-pound barbell over his head. None of these did Calvin want to spend his hard-earned money to see.

Instead Calvin bought a twenty-five cent ticket to see a hand-carved miniature village. A classmate had told him about the exhibit. It was all he thought about.

A young man, who looked to be about seventeen, took everyone's tickets. They were ushered inside the tent and up the steps to the platform where the little village was displayed.

Everyone was instructed not to reach across the rope or touch anything. They had only a short time to walk around the village. In order to see it all, they would need to keep moving.

There was very little light inside the tent, and Calvin was determined to get his money's worth.

He was fascinated with the tiny wires that were attached to the meticulously carved figures. It was the most intriguing thing he had ever seen.

The teenage boy wore a top hat and a white shirt with red suspenders, and spoke through a megaphone. The megaphone wasn't necessary, but it did make him more imposing. Calvin noticed he didn't talk or look like anyone around these parts. He was quite the showman. He took his job seriously, making sure everyone appreciated what they were seeing.

The young man shared many details about the man who carved the village. He said it was made from discarded apple boxes. The entire exhibit had taken over five years to complete. It was built to a one-inch scale, one inch equaling one foot.

Once he had everyone's attention, he flipped a switch with dramatic flair and shouted, "Behold one of the great wonders of the world!"

Calvin gasped! The miniature village came alive! It lit up like a Christmas tree. Tiny lights came on in all the houses, stores, and streets. A hundred little people and animals began moving simultaneously. The sawmill workers started loading logs onto the carriage to be cut with a tiny saw blade that actually turned.

All the little figures began moving. A couple of children on a seesaw were going up and down. A farmer was stacking hay, and a woman milked a cow. The viewers were told again they had only a short time to see the exhibit, so they needed to keep moving.

Calvin was mesmerized and tried to get as close as possible without touching anything. He wanted to see what was used to make hands move, legs walk, and wheels turn. Before he had made it only about halfway around, the young man said, "Thank you, ladies and gentlemen! Please exit to your right."

Calvin was devastated! He couldn't believe his time was already up. He asked the young man if he could stay a little longer. The boy suggested that if he gave him fifteen cents more, he would let him stay through the next showing. He noticed the boy put the coins in his pocket and then nodded at Calvin. "I'll make sure you see everything before the next group is allowed in."

Calvin was impressed with the young man. His accent was different from anyone he had ever heard speak. The tall blond boy appeared to be from a foreign country. He told Calvin his family came by ship from Germany before the war broke out. His father wanted to escape from the crazy man, Adolf Hitler, and didn't want to become a Nazi.

He allowed Calvin to crawl underneath the platform to see the gasoline motor which powered the generator, which made everything work. There were so many gears and pulleys with tiny wires running through small holes in the floor. These were attached to hands and feet.

Calvin noticed the miniature village was on a flatbed trailer. All they had to do was pull the village from town to town. Calvin asked how he knew so much about the little village. The boy said that he and his daddy had made it.

His dad was in an accident and was paralyzed from the waist down. He lost his job at a sawmill and had six kids to feed. Since he was the oldest child, he helped his daddy with the project. His dad still had use of his hands and a talent for carving. The boy said his dad also taught him how to carve the little people.

Calvin was so envious. He wished someone would teach him to carve. The boy said his father would always say, "If you have something that people will pay money to see, you will never go hungry."

The young man traveled with the carnival and represented his family and their financial interest.

Calvin was so impressed. He promised himself that one day he would make a miniature village like the one he had seen at the fair. He looked at his little wooden figure; he had a long way to go.

In the weeks to come, Calvin helped the preacher with fishing. He became good at running the trotlines and checking traps, allowing the old man to stay at camp.

The preacher cooked or smoked gar for Truman, and now there was time for just resting on the porch. He enjoyed their company very much, especially the young boy's energy. Calvin was always one step ahead of what the preacher needed done. Life was good.

He loved to listen to the old man's stories and couldn't wait until all the chores were done and supper was over, because then it was time to gather on the porch. The boy and dog would lay on the porch together with Calvin's head propped on the dog's chest. Penny would perch on the porch railing, while the preacher would rock back and forth in the old rocking chair.

Preacher Joe was in his element. He could spin a tale like no other and relished an appreciative audience. He took great pains in selecting the stories greatly embellished over time—but mostly based on true facts. Calvin had his doubts about some, but, nevertheless, all were spellbinding.

"Brother Calvin, I noticed yuh don't laugh uh lot, so I'm gone 'a tell yuh uh story 'bout why yuh should."

Calvin hadn't realized he didn't laugh very much, but shrugged it off to the fact there hadn't been a whole lot to laugh about in his short life. However, it sounded like an intriguing story, so he chuckled a little, hoping to help the preacher to get on with it.

Preacher Joe took out his Prince Albert can, filled his pipe, struck a kitchen match, and held it to the bowl. He made a few quick puffs, took a long draw, tilted his head back, and let the smoke find its natural release from his puckered lips.

"When I wuz uh young'un 'bout yo age, I went wid my mamma ta uh neighbor's house. I just set down on de do' steps while momma went in.

"Thu woman uf de house had big bones and wuz strong as uh ox. She worked de whole place by herself, 'cause her husband died an' she didn't have no young'uns. Just her an' her hundred-year-ol' daddy lived in de house.

"My momma told me de ol' man didn't have no legs 'cause he had thu diabetes, an' dey had ta cut dem off above thu knees.

"He wuz uh li'l man anyhow and now didn't weigh mor'en fifty pounds. All his hair wuz gone. He didn't have uh hair on 'im an' didn't have uh tooth in his head. His skin wuz kind'a gray color but smooth as uh baby's butt. All thu ol' feller could do wuz just lie on de bed an' try not ta die.

"The daughter had ta work de place by herself. She didn't have no help, so ever' mornin' she'd git 'im out uh de bed, clean 'im up, an' put uh diaper on 'im. She'd feed 'im breakfast, den put 'im on her hip an' take 'im ta de fields an' work.

"He couldn't talk none, so she give him uh little bell ta ring when he'd need sump tin'. She'd set 'im under uh shade tree while she'd work de crops."

The preacher would glance at Calvin from time to time to see if his tale was having the desired effect. As usual, the boy was completely absorbed, so he continued on.

"I's just sit'n thar, mindin' my business, when de screen do' flew open. Thu big-boned woman an' mamma come out on thu porch. De big-boned woman hollered fo me ta come in de house an' see de ol' man. I just shuck my head no, when my momma reach down an' grab me by de ear.

"Boy, git in dis house an' look at her ol' daddy. She wants ta sho yuh how clean he is, an' he don't smell bad, 'cause she keeps 'im so clean just like's uh baby. 'Sides, yuh might never git uh chance ta see another hundred-year-ol' man again.

"So she drags me in de house with de help uf thu big-boned woman. Dey set down at de table an' told me ta goes on in de bedroom an' look at de ol' man. I didn't want ta, 'cause I's 'fraid ta look at 'im . . . Yuh never knows what might hap'en, I thought.

"Deys keep on hollerin' at me ta go in, so I finally open de do', just so's I could peek in. It wuz so dark I couldn't see nut 'en."

"Mamma say, 'Yuh better go in befo' I take uh switch ta yo hind end.'

"I opened de do', just nuff ta squeeze in an' plaster myself up 'gin'st da wall. Thu room wuz dark, even do' it's only de middle uf de day. Dey had shades on de winders. My eyes finely git use ta de dark. All I could see wuz de's li'l ol' bald head sticking out from under dat white sheet.

"His eyes wuz closed, an' I looked an' looked, but I couldn't see 'im breathing. He never moved uh muscle. I's thinking ta myself, he mays be uh hundred, but he didn't make it ta uh hundred an' one.

"Den 'bout that time uh skinny arm with uh boney finger wuz motionin' me ta come over thar. I froze ta de floor and couldn't make uh step. Den all uf uh sudden dat li'l bald head turned t'ward me an' open one eye. Ta des day, I don't know why, but I walked over ta de bed an' just stood thar, not know'n what ta do.

"Quicker'n uh snake, he grab me by de wrist. I scream fer dear life but couldn't get 'im off, so's I start pullin' 'im. I almost had 'im off de bed. He had me with one hand an' wuz trying to hold on to de bedstead with de other.

"Den first thang I knowed, he start howlin' with laugher. He wuz quiet as uh church mouse, den start laughin' so loud dat it made me scream even louder. I just 'bout to jerk 'im off de bed, when thu do' flew open an' de women folk come runnin' in.

"Thu big-boned women wuz hollerin, 'Lord, help us. What's goin' on in here?' Then she come over an' grabbed his wrist an' pulled 'im off me. She's say, 'Daddy, behave, why would yuh scare des boy like dat?'

"She bent over an' picked 'im up an' put 'im on her hip.

"He had dat little ol' bald head throwed back, an' I ain't never heard such laughin' in my life. He had tears an' snot runnin' everywheres. He wuz laughin', de daughter wuz laughin', my momma wuz laughin', everybody laughin' but me!

"De sight uf dat li'l ol' baby man wid uh diaper on cause me ta scream a'gin an' run out thu do'. If he's hadn't turn me lose, I wud uh drugged dat li'l ol' hundred-year-ol' rascal all de way home.

Calvin lost his breath. He had never laughed so much in his entire life.

Then Preacher Joe said, "Just goes ta sho that if yuh laugh uh lot, yuh can lives ta be uh hundred years ol'."

After one of the preacher's stories, Calvin liked to try and figure out how much was actually true and how much was made up. He thought the hundred-year-old baby man story had to be mostly true, because nobody could make that up.

They sat for a long time after the story. There was little talking; both weren't used to talking to other people. Calvin talked to Truman, and the preacher talked to himself and Eller. At times, this made Calvin uncomfortable.

He was afraid he might travel too far to the other plane and may not be able to return.

Calvin decided it might help if he were able to talk to him about his wife.

"Brother Joe, how long ago did your wife die?" he asked.

The old man seemed startled, turned to Calvin, and said, "I has uh daughter. She lives up north. She wants ta come git me and take me out 'a de swamp." He got up from the rocking chair and went to bed.

CHAPTER 18

Faulty Suspenders and Stripped Underwear

Next morning, Calvin woke to the smell of biscuits on the stove and the preacher talking to Truman on the porch. He was a little worried about the old man, but for now things seemed fine.

Calvin had hot biscuits and eggs for breakfast, then went about doing chores for Brother Joe. He wanted to help as much as possible to show appreciation for their food and shelter.

"Let's go, boy! It's fishin' time!"

Preacher Joe, Calvin, and Truman pretty much filled the cypress boat; so they strung their catch on the side of the boat. With the extra weight, it was a struggle for the little three horsepower outboard motor to move against the current.

Calvin helped out paddling now and then on either side. The nose of the old boat never touched the bank before Calvin leaped onto the landing ramp. He would tie it up, grab the stringer, and pull the heavy fish onto the little dock.

Truman, with one leap, was on the bank and bounding up the steps to the porch.

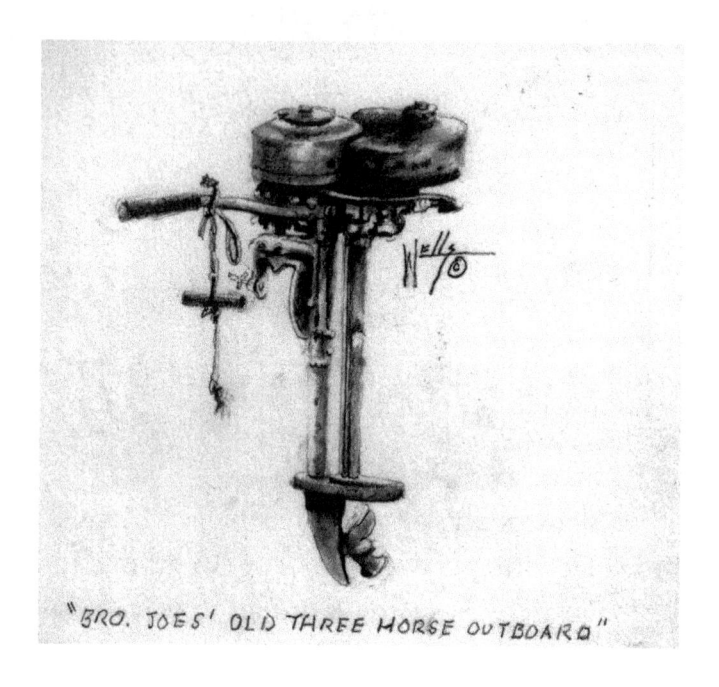

"BRO. JOES' OLD THREE HORSE OUTBOARD"

The old preacher was a little stiff from being in the boat all morning and reached out a hand for Calvin to pull him up.

"Hey, look, Brother Calvin, got uh note in de jar. Fetch it fer me, would yuh?" asked the preacher.

Calvin had to stand on tiptoe and still could barely unscrew the lid to take out the paper. It looked like the note was written on part of a brown paper bag.

The old man slowly walked up the steps, followed by Calvin, and sat down in his rocker. He unfolded the note and seemed to struggle to make out what was written. After a while, he stood up, put the paper in his pocket, and went inside.

For the next few days, the old preacher didn't seem himself. Calvin contributed it to the change in the weather.

Days were getting shorter and cooler, and the fishing was becoming slower.

Once the fishing began to slow, Calvin wondered how long it would be before Preacher Joe would shut the camp down for the season. He didn't want to bring it up. The thought of saying good-bye to the old man wouldn't be easy. He knew he would probably never see him again. Calvin decided not to think about that and just enjoy the time they had left at the old fish camp.

The mornings were beginning to feel a little cool to his bare feet. Calvin asked Preacher Joe if he could help him make a pair of moccasins out of the small canvas.

"I can do better den dat. We'll make yuh some shoes out 'a cowhide. I got some left after put' n a new bottom in my ol' rocker," he said.

They worked on them for several days, trying to soften the cowhide. They put lard on the leather and rubbed it with a rock. The fibers in the leather began to break down, and it became as soft as cloth.

Calvin stood on the leather while the preacher traced the outline of each foot. They made the upper part to fit above the ankle. This would keep his feet dry in a few inches of water. Once the soles were measured and cut, they did the same for the tops. They then took long strips of leather and laced them together.

"Well, go head put 'em on. Let's see how dey fit."

Calvin slipped his feet into the homemade shoes, laced them up, and danced around. He was popping his palm to his mouth, making whooping sounds like an Indian doing a war dance.

That tickled the preacher. It was great to hear the old man laugh again. Calvin knew there was something bothering him, so whenever he could make him laugh, it was good.

His new moccasins were a comfort for Calvin. Now there was one less thing to be concerned about with the coming winter.

Calvin had other concerns: he could barely get into his coat, and his khaki pants were tight. There were a couple more inches of wrist and ankle showing. He had two pairs of long handles that would help with layering in order to stay warm.

When he wore his long handles, shirt, and pants, there was no way he would be able to get into his coat. Sooner or later, he would have to address that problem, but for now his new moccasins were making such a difference with the cooler weather.

It was good to see the preacher sitting on the porch smoking his pipe. At the moment, he didn't seem to have a care in the world. Calvin joined him. For a long while, they just enjoyed the sounds of the river while watching Truman chase a frog along the bank.

"Brother Joe, do yuh miss preaching?" asked Calvin. The old man caressed his beard while his eyes were fixated on the distant horizon.

"Well, ta tells de truth, I never wuz no real preacher. I wern't ordained or nut'n, just spoke uh few times at de church. Mostly just gave my testimony on hows de Lord saved uh sinner likes me ta anybody dat wud listen.

"I don't read all dat good, but over the years I purdy much memorized de Sermon on the Mount. 'Sides I preach all de time.

"Just de yuther day, sit'n on de bank pole fish'n, dare wus uh bunch uh turtles on uh log. I just let 'em have it. I wuz given 'em hellfire and brimstone, and dey just couldn't take it no mo. Dey baled off dat log right an' left. Guess I hit uh soft spot.

"Like my ole grandma told de preacher one time. He wuz preachin' 'bout drunkards and reprobates, an' she wuz amenin' ever word. Den he says somethin' 'bout dip'n' snuff. She told 'im dat he done stopped preachin' an' started medlin'!"

He threw that wonderful old bald head back and let out a thunderous bellow.

Calvin just smiled, not really sure he understood what he was talking about.

"Speakin' uf church, wuz yuh uh church-goin' boy, back at thu foster home?"

"Yes, sir, I went ta Midway Baptist, but I got in uh little trouble one time. Then Mrs. Poole made me sit by her. I couldn't sit with thu other boys. From then on, it wasn't much fun. She said it wasn't supposed to be fun," Calvin pined.

"Sho nuff, how in thu world did yuh git in trouble in thu Lord's House?" The old man smiled.

"One time I was sittin' on thu back pew during uh revival. It was the middle of winter. Thu deacons thought it was goin' ta get really cold that night, so they had both fireplaces roaring by thu time everybody got there, but thu cold spell never showed up.

"It was so hot it took my breath away. I was sitting next ta uh window, so I raised it uh little, so I could breathe.

"The revival preacher was uh short, bald, chubby man, an' he worked up uh sweat in no time. He had ta take his coat off an' lay it on the pew behind him. His suspenders were stretched so tight over his big belly they looked like they might pop off any minute.

"All thu womenfolk were working their fans, trying ta cool off uh little. I was so far back I couldn't understand what thu preacher was talking 'bout an' got bored.

"I noticed red wasps were crawling through thu cracks in thu walls. They must have thought, spring had sprung, it was so hot. One lit on my leg. I stuck my finger out, an' he just crawled on it, didn't try ta sting me, or nothing.

"I took uh ravel off my red socks, 'bout three feet long, an' tied it around his waist. I made him my pet. He would crawl up ta my knee, then take off like uh little airplane off uh runway. I would just pull him back an' let him do it again.

"Some of thu kids saw what I was doin' an' started leanin' over their pew ta watch. They were jealous of my little pet. They wished they had one, but they didn't, so they just watched me play with mine.

"I got uh little careless an' accidently let thu end of thu string go. Thu wasp had warmed up pretty good, 'cause he took off, draggin' his string across thu heads an' backs of everybody. Folks began slappin' at thu string 'cause it tickled thu back of their necks. The congregation started pointin' at thu strange sight.

"It was hard for my little wasp ta fly with that long string tied on him. He was flappin' his wings as fast as he could, makin' a loud buzzin' sound. He finely made it ta thu center aisle. All thu kids started laughin' an' some of the grownups too, but Mrs. Poole was lookin' at me, an' she wasn't laughin'.

"Next thing I knew, thu wasp was headed straight for thu lightbulb hangin' over thu preacher's head.

"'Bout that time thu preacher saw thu wasp, with uh long red string tied to it, coming straight toward him. He couldn't take his eyes off him. He forgot what he was preachin' 'bout an' started swattin' at my wasp but missed ever' time.

"My wasp pet was getting' tired, pullin' that long string. He just couldn't fly no more, so he landed on thu preacher's bald head.

"He grabbed thu string an' slammed my little red wasp ta thu floor an' stomped him with his big foot. When he did, one of them suspenders snapped, an' thu other one couldn't stand thu strain. When it flew off that big belly, his pants dropped straight ta his ankles. He's just standin' there in his gray-striped silk underwear.

"Then thu whole congregation started laughin', all but Mrs. Poole. It all ended up good, though, well for everybody except my little red wasp."

The old preacher was laughing so hard he could barely speak, but managed to ask, "How's that?"

"'Cause thu revival preacher reached down, pulled his pants up with one hand, an' held on for dear life. He used thu other hand ta point at folks and pound thu podium, makin' them feel ashamed for laughin' in church.

"They said it was the best sermon he ever preached. There were nine kids, an' three grownups walked thu aisle. One of 'um was a seventy-eight-year-old woman. They had to help her down to the podium.

"It became known as thu Red Wasp Revival. Maybe you heard of it." Calvin smiled.

Calvin was pleased with himself. The preacher was holding his side, tears flowing from his eyes, bouncing up and down, but only making a squealing sound. There was nothing Calvin enjoyed more than hearing Brother Joe laugh.

CHAPTER 19

The Turning Point

The autumn season had been wonderful for Calvin. The stay at the fish camp with the old preacher had truly been a blessing. Once they left the Tensas River Bottom, in the segregated south, their relationship would not or could not ever be the same again. They both knew and accepted it, but also knew nothing would ever take away their friendship and their time together at the fish camp.

One evening after supper, Calvin stood up and said, "Brother Joe, I want yuh ta baptize me in thu river."

The small congregation gathered at the water's edge. With the sun slowly descending, it cast a golden gleam on the small congregation, consisting of four of God's more unique creations. Truman and Penny looked on from the bank as the preacher dipped the boy under the muddy waters of the Tensas.

Calvin awoke to the sound of scratching and a soft clucking sound. Penny was hovering next to his head. She was not so subtle at trying to wake him up.

He propped on one elbow and looked around. The fire had not been tended, and the coal oil lamp wasn't lit. He didn't know the time but sensed it was much too early for even the preacher to be up.

Calvin sat quietly trying to pick up a familiar sound—the preacher talking to Truman or the little three horsepower motor.

He walked out on the porch in his long handles. The darkness was cold and wet against his face. The silence gave him an uncomfortable feeling. He wanted to call out but was afraid of not getting a response. All of a sudden, he heard a noise. Something was running through the thick brush coming from downriver.

Calvin stood there trying to get his eyes to focus on the source of the racket, getting closer and closer. He knew it must be Truman, but was still startled when he burst from the darkness and bounded up the steps.

"Hey, boy, where yuh been?" asked Calvin. Truman was wet and muddy from head to toe. "Where's Brother Joe?" As though the dog could tell him.

Calvin went inside to put his overalls on, when he noticed the note Preacher Joe had crumpled up lying on the floor next to the table. He smoothed the note out, which read . . .

> Preacher Joe,
> Your family fears for your safety; they say you are too old to be by yourself, and they want us to come get you. Be ready.
>
> Sheriff Walker

So that's why he's been down lately—his daughter's having him picked up.

After getting dressed, he slipped his moccasins on, lit the lantern, and went down to the dock. The boat was gone.

He checked the fish pen by holding the lantern over the top. He could tell by the movement of the water it still was full of fish.

He decided to call out for Brother Joe a couple of times. There was no response. His mind was racing with negative thoughts. The preacher was old, perhaps older than he said he was. Anything could have happened, but one thing was for sure: he was gone.

By now there was a little light, as the sun was trying to top the eastern tree line. Calvin caught a glimpse of the jar hanging on the rope. It looked like there was something inside. He stood on tiptoes and retrieved the note. Once inside, he sat at the table and read by the light from the lantern.

> Brother Calvin,
> Gone to see Eller. Stay as long as yuh want.
> Take what yuh want. Don't need it no mo.
>
> Yo brother in de Lord,
> Preacher Joe

It was clear now why the old man had not been himself since he had gotten the note. He knew Brother Joe had no intentions of going anywhere with the sheriff. The only thing he could do now was try to find him.

He called Truman, hitched him to the cart, and loaded what staples were left. Penny hopped on Truman's back, and the search began. The plan was to go upriver first looking for any sign of Preacher Joe. If he didn't find him, then they'd turn south and continue the search.

After several days, Calvin's little search party reconciled themselves to the fact: they weren't going to find Brother Joe. Either he wasn't there, or he didn't want to be found. Calvin tried not to think about all the bad things that could have happened, but in reality, that was all he thought about.

The note said he was going to see Eller. What did that mean? Calvin knew the preacher didn't want to go up north and live with his daughter, but even Calvin knew he was getting too old to live in the swamp by himself. He hoped he had gone back to his little house and the sheriff would leave him alone. Brother Joe could spend the winter, then maybe come back to the river next year, and they could fish together again.

The earth was tilting on its axis, causing the days to become shorter and colder. Squirrel hunting had become easier now that there were fewer leaves on the trees. It was difficult for them to hide.

When Truman treed a squirrel, he would always stay on the opposite side of the tree as Calvin would circle it looking for any movement. On signal, Truman would grab a sapling and shake it, making the rodent turn toward Calvin.

Calvin's skills with his bow had become deadly as long as the prey was in range. If the tree was too tall, the squirrel would just keep climbing until he was too high. They would move on, hoping for a shorter tree.

Small birds were always available. He would put several on a stick and roast them over the fire. Calvin had reached the point after leaving the fish camp that food was only for survival, the taste wasn't that important.

Acorns were now plentiful, as well as, wild pecans. Both Calvin and the squirrels were harvesting nuts. There were times he would kill a cat squirrel or two and gather nuts at the same time. The acorns made good meal, but he had to soak them in water until the bitter taste was gone. Acorn meal was good, but the process was time-consuming.

Calvin missed the pampered life with the preacher at the camp. There was no worry about food. He missed sitting on the porch, listening to his stories. Calvin feared he would never see him again. Wherever he was, he hoped all was well.

CHAPTER 20

The Flood

The weather had become unpredictable. Some days were mild, and others were cold and rainy. With winter coming, there seemed to be an urgency in everything he did. He wasn't sure why, but he didn't want to make a permanent camp. He would just sleep in the cart and keep moving.

Calvin was a little apprehensive about the coming changes in the weather and his ability to adapt to the cold. He thought it was probably late October and there had been only a few cold days.

Late one afternoon, a front started moving in. The wind began to blow, and dark clouds formed low on the horizon. Occasionally, the wind would catch the canvas on the cart just right and almost rip it off. Truman was putting some shoulder into it to keep on moving.

Calvin noticed a large root ball from a blown-over oak tree that had been uprooted during the hurricane a couple of years ago. The roots were cantilevered away from the trunk. Underneath it would be a good place to park the cart for the night.

There were hot coals in his bucket from his last fire, so he hurried to gather firewood before the rain started. There were a couple of gar fish left from an earlier catch. Calvin put both on a stick near the fire so they would cook slowly and well enough, so the many tiny bones could easily be removed.

After supper, Calvin prepared for the cold rainy night. He gathered more firewood in order to keep a fire going, as long as possible, underneath the root canopy. While dragging logs and limbs to the cart, he once again noticed the high-water marks on the trees from previous floods. There was debris hanging as high as ten feet over his head.

Calvin placed several logs in the hole created when the tree fell knowing it would fill with water if there was a heavy rain. He then pulled the cart on top of them and tied the cart wheels to the underside of the roots.

A third of the roots were still in the ground where it appeared other varmints had wallowed out a burrow for shelter. This would be a good place for Truman. He emptied the cart and placed everything under the root's canopy and climbed in, thinking it would be a sleepless night. Calvin didn't need to worry about Penny. She could fend for herself.

The rain started. Strong winds blew torrents of water underneath the overhanging roots. The cart shook with the impact. During flashes of lightning, Calvin peeked through the canvas and could see that Truman and Penny were both dry. At some point, she had made her way into the burrow with Truman.

They were all safe and dry for the moment, but he began thinking of what the morning light would reveal.

Most of the heavier rain seemed to be up river, so the extent of the flood may not be realized immediately. Calvin only dozed a little overnight, uneasy about a possible flood, but there wasn't anything he could do until morning.

With the first morning light, there was a feeling of dread as Calvin pulled the tarp back. At first his mind couldn't comprehend what he was seeing. It took a moment, but Calvin soon realized they were completely surrounded by water. It had rained hard all night long. He knew they were in a grave situation.

Truman had abandoned his original sanctuary underneath the root ball and was splashing around trying to find a high point above the water level. Calvin slipped his moccasins on because he would now be wading around in cold knee-deep water. Truman came bounding toward Calvin, splashing water everywhere, when he saw him putting everything back in the cart.

"Come on, boy. We got ta get tuh higher ground!" shouted Calvin.

It was all he and Truman could do to keep the cart moving. The peephole Calvin had cut in the floor was leaking a little. The wheels only occasionally touched the ground. It was more like pulling a boat with wheels.

They headed for what seemed to be a little island still above the floodwater. Penny followed along by flying from tree to tree, occasionally dropping down on the cart. He and Truman struggled to reach the little mound of dirt, dragging the cart onto the only patch of visible earth.

Calvin collapsed on the wet ground, trying to get his breath. Even Truman was breathing hard. Calvin knew the water was rising fast and the little island would soon disappear. The water on the ground was from last night's rain, but the floodwater from the heavier rain further north was on its way.

Calvin scanned the trees for the high-water mark. Even on the mound, the floodmark was at least eight feet above his head. There was no way to out run it now. He had known from the start, sooner or later, the time would come when he would have to survive a major flood.

Months ago, he had come up with a plan, and now they would probably all drown if it didn't work.

Calvin needed to find a tree, easy to climb, that had horizontal limbs above the floodmark in order to lay horizontal poles.

After finding such a tree, he quickly cut poles about three inches in diameter and laid them across the level limbs. Calvin constructed a platform about six feet by six feet.

He emptied the cart and took his clothes and what staples he had taken from Brother Joe's camp. They were safely wrapped in the small canvas. He made sure to get the little tub, putting the syrup bucket inside.

Calvin threw the spear onto the platform. He tied both the canvas and the tub with the heavy cord, placing it over his shoulder. Then he climbed the tree. The water was now a few inches over the top of the mound and rising fast.

Calvin climbed back down and hurried back to the cart. He took the long and the short rope from the cart, tying a loop on both. The short rope was slung over his head and shoulders. Next, he climbed a nearby tree and tied the long plowline around the trunk, about twenty feet high. He pulled the other end of the rope up, throwing it over a limb that extended above the platform.

He scampered down and tied the short rope to a front wheel, then looped it through the spokes of the back wheels. Calvin tied the loose end to the other front wheel. He used a long stick to reach the end of the rope hanging over the limb above the platform and pulled it down. Calvin lifted both sides of the short rope up, so they extended about three feet above the cart, and tied the end of the long rope to them.

The water was now knee-deep when he pulled the canvas back and began to try to get Truman into the cart. The water was rising faster, and the cart was practically floating again. Truman's survival instincts kicked in, and he suddenly decided to get into the cart on his own.

Calvin grabbed the double-bit ax and began whaling away at the tree where the long rope was tied. The notch where he had started cutting was now underwater. With every swing of the ax, water splashed him in the face.

All of a sudden, it twisted to the side and split off, still attached to the stump. Down went the treetop, and up went the cart with its occupant inside. It stopped with a sudden jolt, as it reached its apex. The cart began to swing violently back and forth, banging against the platform. Calvin held his breath. He could tell the big dog was nervous and was about to jump. His ears were flapping as he turned his head in all directions at once.

Looking up, Calvin cupped his hands around his mouth and shouted, "No, boy. Stay! It's okay!"

As the cart became more stable, Truman slowly sat back down, and Calvin breathed once again.

The water was now chest high, but somehow he made it to the base of the tree just as the floodwater began to sweep him off his feet. He struggled to climb with the ax in his hand. The water had risen so quickly; it was only about four feet from the bottom of the horizontal logs. He threw the ax on top and, with all the strength he had left, pulled himself up.

Once the cart stopped swinging, Truman leaped from the cart onto their perch in the tree. He looked as though he was thinking about bailing off and trying to swim for dry land, but Calvin calmed him down.

"It's okay, boy." He kept repeating in his ear while holding him around his neck. They were both shivering: Calvin from the cold water and Truman from being fifteen feet up in a tree. Their tiny crow's nest was now perched above a vast reservoir as far as the eye could see.

The river had become a boiling, swirling, muddy mass of brown sludge. Huge logs were moving downriver. They were jerked under by the violent current, then shot straight up. It was a terrifying sight. Calvin realized how fortunate they were not to have already been consumed by this monstrous body of destruction.

Calvin had already witnessed several deer, wild hogs, and numerous smaller animals floating past. Snakes were seeking refuge in trees, trying to fight the strong current.

The tree Calvin and Truman were in was being pushed around. Logs were bumping into the trunk, and it began shaking from the water surges.

The sheer force of nature was hard for him to comprehend. Enormous waves were pushing volumes of water further into the swamp and away from the river's normal boundaries.

After making sure Truman wasn't going to jump off their small sanctuary, Calvin felt the need to get the cart secure. A log had just hit the plowline and caused the cart to fly up and slam into the limb it was looped over. The cart fell back down with a jerk. That was the one thing he hadn't considered.

He had planned to wait until the water receded, then slowly let the cart down by holding the end of the rope. Now he realized at any moment the rope could be broken and the cart would be thrown into the flood waters.

Calvin had two major problems: the cart and the fact he was freezing. He was wet from head to toe, so getting warm took priority. Hypothermia was a possibility. He had to get dry clothes on in a hurry.

Calvin took his soaking wet moccasins off and hung them on a limb to dry. He stripped down and managed to control the shaking long enough to untie the canvas and put on his dry shirt and overalls.

He had matches from the cabin, and hopefully he could find something that would burn. There was still a jar of cotton balls with Vaseline inside the small canvas. Calvin cut limbs off the tree they were in and started a small fire in the foot tub. Fortunately, it was a mild day in November, and it didn't take long for him to feel his temperature begin to rise.

He and Truman sat by the fire while he tried to assess their dilemma. He was grateful that they had survived to this point, but he knew they were still in a lot of trouble. Calvin decided to take his chances and hope the cart would still be hanging in the tree in the morning. There was another problem to take care of.

The poles they were on weren't secure. If he stepped too close to the end, it could flip up or slip off. He used some of the heavy cord and wrapped it around the ends of the poles, then tied the cord to the limb. He repeated the process on the other side. They still moved a little when walked on but should stay in place.

Calvin's concentration was broken for a moment by a loud cackling in the cart. He felt a little guilty as this was the first time he had thought about Penny since the flood started. The fact that she could fly gave her a distinct advantage of surviving over him and Truman. Under these circumstances, it was everyone for himself.

Penny was letting the boys know she had just laid an egg and had been keeping an eye on them at the same time.

Calvin was able to stand on tiptoe, grab the cart tongue, and pull it toward him just enough to reach the egg. He rolled it up in his wet shirt and placed it in the small canvas. The little egg wasn't enough to eat by itself, so he would save it to use in fry bread.

Trapped on a small six-by-six-foot platform, the quest for food would become their constant endeavor. Calvin had seen several drowned animals floating past. They could have been food, but there was no way to salvage them.

He had several pounds of flour and about the same amount of meal, lard, a little baking soda, salt, and pepper that he had taken from the fish camp. He had two gallons of drinking water left in his canvas water bag. Truman and Penny would drink floodwater. This wouldn't be a problem for them. It was deadly for Calvin.

He knew it would take several days for the water to recede back to the banks of the Tensas. The swamp would be a muddy mess for several more days. Fishing would be almost impossible until things got back to normal. He would have to rely on every skill and instinct he had to survive until the floodwater was gone.

It was a long night. The logs continued to float past their perch; neither he nor the dog slept. Truman stood with his front paws lapped over the edge of the platform. They watched hour after hour trying to see what was passing them in the dark.

The morning light brought with it a heavy fog. It was an eerie feeling standing in the middle of an immense body of brown water and not being able to see more than a few feet in any direction.

The water wasn't moving as fast as it had been, but it was still difficult to see floating debris until it was right on them.

Calvin took his spear and began to push heavy water-soaked logs away from their platform. He had seen other trees fall over, when a log slammed into it and realized the possibility of their tree doing the same. The ground was soaked; the roots could give way and over they would go.

He and Truman had stationed themselves facing upriver in order to intercept anything large enough to do damage to their lodging. Through the mist, they both saw it at the same moment.

A huge tree—limbs, root ball, and all—was slowly moving downriver. Its downstream journey was interrupted only when it crashed into a tree. It either pushed them over, or the strong current forced it to change direction. This was certainly large and heavy enough to push their tree over. It was headed straight for their refuge.

The moss-laden limbs reached well above their platform. Calvin knew there would be little he could do if its course didn't change. The tree limbs could literally pull the platform from underneath them.

Calvin watched closely as the tree moved with the current. He was convinced it wouldn't be a direct hit, but some limbs were definitely going to make contact with the poles they were sitting on. The only thing he could do was try to help them pass by, without them doing too much damage.

Calvin readied himself with his spear, as a large branch draped with Spanish moss made contact. It rocked the tree backward, knocking him to his knees. He grabbed hold of the trunk and held on until the tree stopped swaying. Still on his knees, all Calvin could see was a dark mass of moss and what appeared to be two beady eyes peering at him.

The hair on Truman's back stood up. He made a low growl as he locked in on those two eyes embedded in the black mask. The huge floating tree stalled for a moment.

Cautiously, Calvin used the tip of his spear to push some of the moss aside. The masked bandit flew from his cover, hitting Calvin's shoulder, then ricocheted on to the back of the big dog. There the varmint bowed up and sunk his needlelike teeth.

Truman began spinning around on the small platform, grabbing at the varmint's tail. Calvin sprung to his feet and began poking the animal with his spear. He was holding on with a death grip until the sharp file point of the spear found a soft spot. For a split second, he loosened his grip to bite at the spear. The big dog flung him to the floor. There is nothing fiercer than a terrified raccoon fighting for his life.

The raccoon arched his back and stood on tiptoe to look as imposing as possible. This worked on Calvin, who was looking for a way to escape, but not the huge dog the raccoon had just bitten.

Now the raccoon would have lost this battle under any circumstances, but for the fact that he had just drawn blood from Super Dog's back gave him zero chance. With a flurry of growls and squeals, it was quickly over.

When survival is your only objective, you take advantage of any opportunity that comes your way. This one actually leaped in their lap and couldn't have come at a better time.

Calvin had eaten raccoon with Mr. Poole many times. It was Walker Poole's favorite wild game. He bragged there was no one in the state of Louisiana that could cook better coon than him.

He would season it well, then roast it slowly in the oven, with sweet potatoes and garlic. It had never been Calvin's favorite. It seemed a little too greasy to him.

He now knew how important fat is for surviving. Most wild game such as rabbit and squirrel have little or no fat. He was told by the Canein' Man how important fat was for his survival. He would eventually die if he only ate lean meat.

After skinning the raccoon, Calvin ran a stick through it and sprinkled it with a little salt and pepper. He let the fire burn down to hot coals in the tub and placed the cast-iron skillet on the coals to catch the grease. He turned the raccoon slowly until it was cooked.

There was still flour and meal left from the fish camp to make some fried bread. He needed a little water and the egg he had saved to hold the flat cakes together.

Calvin tied a five-foot cord to the bale of the syrup bucket, leaned over, and scooped up a full bucket of water. The floodwater wasn't safe to drink, but would be fine for the bread mixture, which he cooked in the hot raccoon grease.

The smell was intoxicating. He and Truman were ravished with hunger. Calvin finally pulled the charred meat off the stick and cut it into pieces. He separated it into piles, giving Truman the most. The bread was fried in the fat and tasted as good as or better than the meat.

Penny dropped down from a limb a few feet above their heads and joined them for dinner. Calvin used the ax to crack the bones so Penny could get to the marrow. This was the least he could do for her since she produced the little brown egg for the fried bread.

They ate well. Calvin ended up with leftovers and a nice hide to clean and scrape.

The next day, Calvin was relieved to see the cart still hanging above their platform. Several times during the night, something would hit the rope. The cart would suddenly rise, then fall quickly as the object made its way past.

Sleeping was difficult. Two nights in a row, with very little sleep and trapped on a small perch made Calvin grumpy. Even Truman seemed somewhat out of sorts. Calvin's mood changed when he saw how much the water had gone down. If it continued at this rate, they would be able to climb down and stand on the little mound of ground by afternoon.

He could then use the platform poles for firewood. They had been very fortunate because of the unusually warm weather for this time of year. He thought it must be late November, and he knew it could change at any moment.

Just before sunset, Calvin put everything back in the small canvas, rolled it up, and threw it to the ground. He dumped some of the coals from the tub into the bucket and lowered it to the ground with the long cord. He then untied the logs, leaving only enough for them to sit on, and threw the rest down for fire wood.

Truman was getting nervous with the whole process. Calvin knew it was time to get him down before he jumped.

They began a less-than-graceful decent down the tree. Calvin went first trying to help place the dog's paws on the right limbs while trying to keep from falling himself. They had made it about halfway, when Truman bailed.

The Goliath dog wasn't built for climbing nor flying for that matter. He hit the wet ground with a thud sliding on his chest, creating a wake of muddy water. The impact knocked his breath out. Fortunately, the ground was soft. Unable to move, he lay flat on the ground, legs going in all directions.

Calvin scampered down and ran over, shouting, "Truman! Are yuh okay, boy?"

He was afraid he had broken a leg or worse. It took a while before Truman could pull himself up. Calvin was examining him all over, trying to make sure there was nothing broken.

"Yuh shouldn't have jumped, yuh big crazy dog! It had ta be at least twelve feet," Calvin said with a trembling voice.

Truman was sitting on his haunches, in somewhat of a daze, but otherwise seemed okay. Calvin sat beside him for a while, hoping he just had his breath knocked out and otherwise would be all right. He didn't think he should coach him into standing until he was ready.

Finally, Truman stood on all fours and walked stiff legged around for a while, as though he was trying to make sure everything was working. It wasn't until he trotted to a stump, hiked a hind leg for a sprinkle, that Calvin gave a sigh of relief. He was fine.

The floodwaters had receded from the high ground beneath the tree, but it was still very wet and muddy. He surveyed the situation. The first thing he needed to do was to start a fire and then get the cart on the ground.

There were matches and cotton balls in the canvas roll. He also had the logs from the platform but needed some kindling. With everything in sight soaking wet, finding small limbs dry enough to start a fire wouldn't be easy.

After looking around he spotted a few limbs caught in trees above the flood line. Calvin took his spear and knocked down an armload of limbs. He placed them on hot coals and after they were burning he threw on logs from the platform and rejoiced in the glorious blaze.

His face flushed warm from the flames. It felt so good! It was the first time he had been warm since he stepped from the cart into the floodwaters two days ago. The unseasonably warm weather had been a blessing, but being wet for the last couple of days was taking its toll.

Once Calvin was warm, he could now focus on something else: his stomach. He hadn't realized how hungry he was until Penny appeared out of nowhere and reminded Calvin that there was at least one egg in the cart. He had seen the little hen on two occasions hop from a nearby tree onto the cart and go inside to lay one of the precious nuggets.

The end of the long plow line was still tied to the wedged tree top. The top of the tree had been wedged against a couple of larger trees by the floodwater, which was the only reason the cart was still there. The idea was to let the cart down slowly without dropping and damaging it.

He chopped the tree trunk into just above the rope. He knew the bottom half should be heavy enough to keep the cart suspended while he chopped the last few fibers attached to the stump. He grabbed the rope where it was tied to the tree. With all his strength, he dragged the tree, inch by inch, toward the cart. This allowed the cart to slowly descend until it was safely on the ground.

Calvin searched inside and was pleasantly surprised to find two small eggs. This afternoon, they would go scavenging around to see what the flood might have left them, but tonight there would be fried bread and leftover raccoon.

For the first time in two days, they were on somewhat dry land. They could sit by the warm fire, have a good meal, and finally be able to sleep in the cart.

It took two more days for the water to recede back to the river banks. On the third day, at the break of dawn, Truman was harnessed up, and they slowly began moving through the dark umber-colored landscape. Calvin felt he was walking on the bottom of a lake that had just been drained. Everything was covered with mud, and some low places were still holding water. It was strange standing on the ground looking up at the mud-coated trees, ten feet over his head.

For the first time he realized that they should not have survived. The stench of death was strong. He spotted a deer carcass hanging from a tree and a couple of bloated hogs floating down the river. Buzzards were moving in, gliding silently overhead, as they looked for the carnage from the flood. He thanked God they were safe and prayed the same for Preacher Joe.

They were slipping and sliding their way south, when Calvin noticed a deep hole of water. Upon closer observation, he noticed black whiskers and white puffy lips, breaking the surface. The hole was full of buffalo and catfish, trapped when the floodwaters receded too quickly for them to make it back to the river. Calvin decided to set up camp and use every means possible to take advantage of the opportunity.

He attached the largest hook he had to the end of a long cane pole, then hooked them under their gills and drug them out. Over the next few days, he took almost all the fish out. Some weighed more than ten pounds.

Calvin quickly put together a smoker using the small canvas and switch cane covered with mud and leaves. He formed a hoop from a long flexible limb and stretched the raccoon pelt on it. He placed the skin in the smoker, along with the fish so it would tan.

They ate fish every meal, along with whatever else they could find. While the smoker was preserving their catch, he searched for anything that would help balance his diet.

Chapter 21

Surviving the Flood

Days after the flood, the bottom was still wet and muddy. He needed to help Truman with the cart, either pulling or pushing. Calvin had strung the smoked fish on the heavy cord and draped it over the cart. This added extra weight. They expended a lot of energy but finally made it to higher ground.

For the next few weeks they lived off the smoke fish along with the staples he took from the fish camp.

The little copper-colored hen, as regular as clockwork, provided an egg for the boys every other day. Calvin would show his appreciation by grinding her some acorns. She liked to peck them from his hand.

Some time had passed after the flood. Calvin knew winter was around the corner. He wasn't sure but thought it had to be late November or early December. This was the first time since arriving in the swamp he awoke to a heavy frost. The golden leaves of autumn were no longer contrasting against a blue sky, but now provided a multi-colored carpet on the ground.

Calvin had outgrown his coat, so he washed the smoke out of the small canvas and made a cloak out of it. He sewed the raccoon pelt on for a collar. The tanning process had made it soft and pliable. He carved a wooden button to fasten it at the neck, cut slits on the sides for his arms, and wore it like a poncho.

The canvas was now so old it was soft and subtle, but was still waterproof. With the raccoon cloak, moccasins, and necklace adorned with boar and alligator teeth, Calvin looked more like an eleven-year-old from the Paleolithic era.

They made their way south but didn't follow the crooks and turns of the river. This time of year, fishing wasn't that productive anyway. He would have to expend too much energy for too little return.

They didn't camp on the riverbank as long as they had a full water bag or a source of good water. He was afraid of being seen. Even though he didn't think people were still looking for Preacher Joe, he had heard gunshots and voices.

This was hunting season. After the floodwaters receded, activity on the river had picked up. He knew duck and squirrel hunters would walk the riverbanks, mostly on the Tallulah side. Still, he needed to be careful.

Calvin found a nice spot to set up camp, which had large oak trees with lots of acorns. Now that the wild grapes and muscadine were gone, there would be very little variety in their diet until spring.

After all the rain, there was a small stream of clean clear water seeping from the underneath side of the mound.

They pulled the cart on top of the bluff. With almost all the leaves now on the ground, he was shocked to see the creek and the bridge that crossed over the Tensas. Calvin knew it existed because he and some of the other boys from the foster home took a shortcut to Vicksburg with Mr. Poole when they took a field trip to the civil war memorial.

It was just a dirt road, but he could hear an automobile rumble across the bridge a few times a day. Calvin felt a little uncomfortable. He could see the river to the east and the dirt road and bridge to the south, and he knew he was only a mile or two from the gravel road behind him that would take him to the bridge he had crossed more than ten months ago. All he had to do was travel south. The River Bottom would continue for another thirty miles or more. He had never spent any time in that area. For all he knew, there may be people living there.

Calvin was experiencing some anxiety for the first time since he left the foster home. He truly didn't know what to do. Things didn't seem as clear to him as they once did. It was his responsibility to make sure he and his companions had food, yet lately it was a struggle to motivate him to do what was necessary to keep them from hunger.

Recently, he had experienced some doubts and for the first time began to second-guess himself. Thoughts of Emily Mae, Mr. Poole, Brother Joe, and his mother and daddy made him realize no matter where he went he couldn't escape those tragic events in his life. He decided to stay on the little mound for a while until he could get himself together.

Calvin had several bad dreams, one after the other. They were about the few people he loved who were no longer with him. The one recurring dream that bothered him the most was of Emily Mae.

The nightmare was always the same. A bright glow would be hovering above him; it was his little sister wearing her white cotton gown with delta mud splattered on it.

She repeated the same thing over and over, "Calvin, yuh promised yuh would never leave me!"

She would persist until he woke up. The guilt was so overwhelming he couldn't get the image out of his mind.

The other dream he had several nights in a row. He would see Brother Joe and a young man working on a barn door. The young man had his back turned toward him. Even though he couldn't see his face, he could tell it was his daddy. He tried desperately to get their attention by shouting louder and louder, but in reality, he couldn't raise his voice above a whisper. He then tried running to them, but his legs were so heavy he couldn't move. It was as if he was in quicksand. When he woke up, the images were gone.

Over the next few days, Calvin seemed to struggle in order to make the simplest of decisions. A front moved in bringing with it cold rain and more melancholy days. Truman would go on hunting trips, and Penny provided for herself, but Calvin found himself doing without, rather than getting out in the cold and rain.

He was surviving on fried bread, rather than hunting. Calvin knew this wasn't good and promised himself to snap out of his stupor. For some reason it persisted. The rain continued, and the decision to stay put was an easy one.

Calvin gathered some firewood and prepared for another cold, rainy night. He built the fire as close to the cart as possible without putting it in danger of catching fire. Lately, he had started placing a round flat rock in the fire. When it was good and hot, he would roll it up in one of the rags he used for a towel, and put it in the cart. It would keep the inside warm until early morning. He also began sleeping with his moccasins on. Staying warm seemed to be more important at the moment than hunting for food.

There was a large smoked buffalo fish left, but Truman found a roadkill rabbit that afternoon. He decided to save the fish for another meal. This was an unexpected benefit to being this close to the road. The serious downside was that he might be seen.

Calvin still had a few staples left from the fish camp consisting of flour, meal, and a cup of lard. He also had some sassafras roots he got from the fish camp that Brother Joe used as medicine.

His stomach seemed a little upset. Mr. Poole use to make the tea for that purpose. For supper, Calvin had the hot tea, a boiled egg, and shared fried bread with Penny.

CHAPTER 22

"Don't Let Go of thu Rope"

There had been rain off and on for the last several days. The river was high, but nothing like it had been during the flood two months ago.

Calvin decided to turn in early, listening to the light but steady rain as it pelted the canvas top. After a bit of digging, Truman managed to scratch a hole and crawl under the cart, which was a tight squeeze. It was going to be a cold night, so Calvin heated up his rock, placing it near his feet, and spread the quilt over him. He left the tarp open, hoping to receive some warmth from the fire, but it was soon doused by the rain.

Calvin wasn't able to go to sleep right off with too much on his mind. He took out his cigar box, which contained his gold watch and fiddled around with the other items inside the box.

There was the rolled diamond back skin. He had planned to make a headband but hadn't got around to it. He had placed the rattles from the Diamond Back on a necklace, but later took them off because they made too much noise when he was trying to slip through the woods.

Also, there was one of the tusks from the wild boar that was never used on his necklace, some big alligator teeth, and the lanyard he had found around Truman's neck.

Wrapped in one of his rags was the carving he had started at the fish camp. It was a little boy wearing overalls. He would give it to Emily Mae if he ever saw her again. Going through the items in his box was somewhat like reading a diary of his adventure.

The watch, by far, was his most prized possession. It always seemed to make him feel better. It was his one connection to a world that he didn't belong to anymore. Calvin once again rubbed the engraved name on the watch, "Hawk Young." His thoughts would always return to his little sister and the guilt he felt for breaking his promise.

Eventually, he drifted into an uneasy sleep. At some point in the middle of the night, Truman crawled out from under the cart, bumping his head. The noise woke him, and Calvin thought he felt himself sitting up.

The rain had stopped, and surprisingly the fire was now blazing. Calvin was startled to see a dark figure silhouetted against the fire. He was petrified, not able to speak, or even move.

The figure was wearing a black hat and overcoat. Truman was standing on his hind legs with his front paws on the man's chest. They appeared to be the same height. The man was talking to him in a low voice while rubbing the big dog's head. He was wearing white gloves.

It was the Canein' Man! Calvin was thrilled to see him and tried to call out, but again wasn't able to make a sound. No matter how hard he tried, he couldn't get his attention.

CALVIN AND THE GREAT TENSAS RIVER BOTTOM

Suddenly, the figure pushed Truman down. He seemed to float to the back of the cart, pulling the canvas back and sticking his head inside. With their faces almost touching, Calvin could make out the pasty skin above the red bandana. He just stared at Calvin for a moment, the handkerchief moving in and out with his breathing.

In a low voice, he said, "Don't let go of thu rope." He placed a white gloved hand over Calvin's mouth so he couldn't speak and disappeared.

Calvin jerked into consciousness. He was still lying flat on his back as though he had never moved at all. For several minutes, he just lay there, reliving what he had just witnessed. Even though it seemed so real, Calvin decided it had to be another strange dream and gradually dozed off to sleep.

"Help! Help!"

Calvin woke hearing these words rising above the sound of rushing water from the Tensas. It was answered by frantic barking from Truman.

Calvin, wearing just his long handles and moccasins, jumped out of the cart. The shouts were coming from the direction of the bridge. It was still early, but there was enough light to make out an image that stopped him in his tracks. Standing on top of a car with only the roof still above water was a man shouting for help.

Truman had been running up and down the bank, barking until he saw Calvin; then he wheeled and ran toward him.

"Come on, boy. We got uh help him!"

They both ran back to the cart. Calvin grabbed the plowline and quickly returned to the edge of the river. It was getting lighter, and he could see the man, wearing black dress pants and a white shirt. He was soaked, barefooted, and shaking uncontrollably.

At first neither spoke; they just looked at each other. The man then said, "The current's too strong. Don't think I can make it."

"I'll tie uh stick on thu end of thu rope, and maybe I can chunk it ta yuh!" shouted Calvin.

"It's worth a try, but I think it's too far," the man said.

Calvin found a heavy water-soaked stick about eighteen inches long and tied it to the rope. Then he tied the other end around his waist. He grabbed the rope a couple of feet from the stick, reared back, and threw it as hard as he could.

The rope landed ten feet short and about the same distance below his target. He tried over and over, never getting close enough for the man to even have a chance to try and catch it.

Calvin moved as close to the edge of the bank as possible in order to shorten the distance. Several times he slipped in as he threw the rope getting his feet wet. Calvin was now as cold as the shivering man he was trying to save. It was obvious to them both: this wasn't going to work.

Disappointment was beginning to show on the man's face, which was now purple from the cold. Calvin wasn't giving up.

The man shouted, "Son, you're worn out! The water is rising, and I feel the car moving! It's going to go at any minute. I have to try and swim for the bank!"

He had been exposed to the cold too long, and the current was too strong. They both knew he wouldn't make it.

Truman was running back and forth on the bank, whining. He would dip a paw in the cold swift water and then take it out as if he was testing it.

Calvin shouted, "Hey, mister! I got uh idea! Don't move! If thu rope's long enough, this might work!"

He retrieved the rope, untied the stick, grabbed Truman by the neck, and made a loop large enough to slip over his head. He made the loop stationary so it wouldn't tighten and choke him.

"Mister, my dog is uh strong swimmer. If thu rope is long enough, he'll make it ta yuh!" shouted Calvin.

He knew this was the last hope. The man gave Calvin a faint smile and nodded his approval.

Calvin took Truman upriver, trying to calculate the angle he would need to account for the swift current. From the corner of his eye, he saw the man stumble as water began running over the top of the car. It was now just a matter of time before the car, along with the person on top, would be swept downriver. The man was beginning to panic, and Calvin knew he had only one shot to get it right.

The big dog was straining against the rope. Calvin showed him the angle. He lunged through the air and hit the water with powerful strokes. Truman displayed amazing strength and agility as he bucked against the swift current.

Calvin saw his calculations were good, but it was now down to the length of the rope. He was running parallel with the dog, trying to keep the rope straight, but that was creating some slack. Truman held his head up and locked on his target. He was now about halfway there.

Calvin and the man were both shouting encouragement to the big dog when he felt the rope hit something, pulling Truman's head under. Calvin's heart sank. The man saw the dog's head go under at the same moment. Calvin could feel Truman struggling against what felt like a submerged limb. He could feel it moving, as the dog lunged to break free.

Truman's head was now completely underwater. Calvin was terrified; he didn't know what to do. It seemed Truman had been under forever.

The man, in a resigned, shaky voice, said, "Son, just let the rope go and save your dog! I'm done for . . . At least give your dog a chance."

Calvin, with cold trembling hands, remembered the words in his dream:

"Don't let go of thu rope."

He was holding as tightly as possible, but felt his grip slipping just as the dog's head popped up only a few feet below the car.

The stranded man had already lay down and pushed off the top of the car. He tried to propel himself forward with his bare feet, causing the car to dislodge and now float downstream. With his support gone, the man instantly realized he wasn't able to swim in the strong current.

However, Truman was swimming in place and actually inching upstream. The drowning man was frantically trying to grasp hold of anything. His hand touched the rope just as the current swept him past the dog.

Calvin quickly tied his end of the rope around a small tree on the bank. The swift water pulled the rope tight, causing the man and dog to swing toward the bank.

The exhausted man was holding on to the rope a couple of feet above Truman's head. When the rope snapped tight, Truman's head pulled out of the loop. This allowed the weakened and now hypothermic man to slip an arm inside the loop and hold on long enough for Calvin to pull him onto the bank.

Calvin was about to take off down the river to look for Truman, when he saw him galloping toward them, choking and coughing up water.

The man was in great danger of dying if he couldn't get warm. He was too out of breath to speak but managed to get to his feet. With Calvin's help, he made it up the hill to the campfire.

Calvin gave him his quilt and went to gather more firewood while the man undressed and wrapped the quilt around his quivering body. He sat on a log and almost stuck his feet and hands into the flames.

Calvin was also cold and wet. He went behind the cart, removed his soaked long handles, and put on dry overalls. He threw his poncho over his head, turned his moccasins upside down to dry, and sat down on the log by the fire.

Truman laid so close to the fire that Calvin thought he smelled the hair on his tail burning, so he reached over with a bare foot and pulled it back. He noticed a slight smile and a bit of twinkle in the man's eye.

"That probably was a good idea. My name is Hudson Clark. I will never be able to thank you and your dog enough. While I was trapped on top of my car, I thought of my wife. She is all I have, and I was afraid I would never see her again."

Calvin was going to ask how he ended up in the river, when he realized the man was overcome with emotion and fighting back tears.

In a broken voice, he said, "I prayed to the Lord he would let someone find me, and he sent you and Samson, the dog. Thank the Lord a lesser dog could have never done what he did. I'm so sorry, son, I haven't even asked your name."

Calvin was about to speak, when Mr. Clark said, "Excuse me," and jumped up, holding the quilt with one hand, putting the other over his mouth; ran barefooted to some bushes; dropped to his knees; and threw up. He stayed there for some time. He had swallowed a lot of the muddy Tensas.

After a while, Mr. Clark stood up, pale as a sheet, and said, "I think I feel a little better." He returned to his seat on the log. "Sorry about that," he said as he sat back down.

Calvin smiled and asked, "How 'bout some hot sassafras tea? It might help."

He put the pot on the coals. Once it started smoking, he poured the tea in his cup and handed it to Mr. Clark. His hands, still shaky, managed to get the warm liquid inside his cold body.

Calvin watched, as the man sipped the warm beverage. He knew this wasn't the typical resident in these parts. He could tell from the roof of the car that it was a new one. Mr. Clark was wearing dress clothes, and Calvin was pretty sure he wasn't on his way to church this time of day. No, this was a businessman.

Most people Calvin knew were working-class people who didn't have much. They were content with their lot in life as long as they had a roof over their head and food on the table. They were happy, but Mr. Clark was different. Calvin could tell he was well educated, but here in the swamp, he was out of his element.

"I just don't know what happened. In my headlights, I saw something strange standing in front of the bridge. The next thing I knew, I'm in the middle of the river, crawling out the window of my car. I was on my way home from a meeting in Baton Rouge. The road was slick. Guess I just slipped off. I should have known it was a mistake to take this shortcut to Vicksburg. I'm sorry I'm just kind of talking to myself. I told you my name. What's yours, young man?"

Calvin was a little hesitant. It was possible he may have heard about a missing boy. Preacher Joe had even heard about it. He finally blurted out, "Calvin, Calvin Young."

"Well, Calvin Young, you have no idea how glad I am to meet you. I heard you call that great dog, Truman, after the president, I presume?"

Calvin just nodded the affirmative.

"I don't know where to start, but I have to ask, what are you doing out here? Do you sleep in that cart? Looks like you've been out here awhile. Why are you living in this swamp? Shouldn't you be in school?"

Calvin just sat there, not knowing which or if he should answer any of this man's questions.

"I apologize, Calvin, there's just so many questions I would like to ask you, but you have just saved my life. You don't have to tell me anything you don't want to. It's really none of my business."

Calvin sat there for a minute, then said, "I'm hungry. Would yuh like something ta eat?"

"I sure would," said Hudson Clark.

"You sit where yuh are, an' we'll let our clothes dry."

Calvin took a piece of cord and strung a clothesline between two saplings close to the fire and hung out their wet clothes.

"I'll make some pancakes an' eggs. I only have one plate. Yuh can have it. I'll eat out of thu skillet," said Calvin. "I have uh little wild honey Brother Joe gave me. I've been saving it, but we'll have it on thu cakes."

Mr. Clark looked around, startled. "Who's Brother Joe?"

Calvin realized he needed to tell his story from the beginning.

He handed Mr. Clark his cakes with wild honey, along with two of the three eggs.

"Thanks, Calvin, I'll wait until yours are done."

"No, sir, eat yours while they're hot," insisted Calvin.

He noticed Mr. Clark bowed his head for a moment before taking his first bite. This told Calvin something else about the man.

"These eggs are wonderful. Where in the world would you get eggs out here?" asked Mr. Clark.

"I've got a little hen. She lays one every other day. Her name's Penny. She's around here somewhere," said Calvin with a smile.

When his cakes were brown on both sides, he broke the small egg on the edge of the skillet. As soon as the sizzle stopped, he took it off the fire.

"It'll cook the rest of the way on this hot skillet," said Calvin and sat on the log by Mr. Clark.

"What about your dog, Truman? Do you have anything for him?"

"I have uh smoked buffalo fish for him. It's thu last one. I've got ta get some traps in thu water. Fish just won't bite in that high muddy water," explained Calvin.

"I rolled everything I owned up in that quilt you're wearing, threw it out thu window, then jumped out after it," said Calvin.

CHAPTER 23

Christmas Eve

When he finished his story, Mr. Clark sat there in stone silence. He couldn't form a word but could only stare at Calvin. Finally, he said, "That's the most incredible story I have ever heard. How old are you, son?"

"Well, I think I'm eleven. How much longer ta Christmas?" asked Calvin.

"That's right. You wouldn't know, would you?" said Mr. Clark. "That's the reason I was in such a hurry to get back from Baton Rouge. Today's Christmas Eve."

Then with a big smile, Calvin said, "I'm twelve."

"Yuh clothes should be dry by now. I'll walk with yuh ta thu road behind us. Take uh right, an' it'll take yuh ta Tallulah," said Calvin.

"How far is that?" asked Hudson Clark.

"It's only 'bout eighteen miles or so. There are folks going up an' down thu road pretty regularly, though. Yuh can hitch uh ride without no problem. Yuh can still spend Christmas with yuh wife," he said, smiling," but yuh better get going."

"Calvin, I just don't know what to say. Are you going to stay here? After hearing your story, maybe you should check on your little sister. Like you say, she probably has been adopted and spending Christmas with her new family, but you will never know for sure unless you go back. That will have to be your decision. No one can make it for you."

Mr. Clark stepped behind some bushes and put on his dry shirt and pants and started to hand Calvin the quilt.

"No, keep it around your shoulders until we get ta thu road. Yuh never know how long it will be before someone comes along. It's only uh couple of miles. I'll hitch Truman ta thu cart, 'cause it's about time we move on anyway."

Calvin slipped on his damp moccasins. Truman pulled the cart off the little mound, and they followed behind. Calvin glanced back and noticed several items not loaded on the cart, but Truman just kept moving forward. He thought to himself he would come back for them after he walked Mr. Clark to the road.

From somewhere above, there was quite a commotion and a small puff of feathers flew down from a nearby tree landing on Truman's back. Mr. Clark was startled by all the cackling.

"Well, this must be Miss Penny." He smiled. "I wondered where she might be. Thanks, young lady, for those two eggs. They had to be the best I have ever eaten!"

They were now in sight of the gravel road to Tallulah, with an old pickup truck coming down the road toward them.

"Someone is coming. Yuh better run," said Calvin.

"I hate to leave you here, Calvin. Please come with me!" shouted Mr. Clark as he tried to run barefooted toward the road.

"I don't think so, but if yuh would, check on my sister for me!" shouted Calvin.

"Okay, I promise," said Mr. Clark.

Then he stopped. "Calvin, I have to tell you something. Remember when I told you I saw a strange sight, and that was the reason I ran off the road into the river."

Calvin nodded yes.

"Well, I guess I was about half asleep, but I swear I saw a man in a black overcoat and hat, wearing white gloves. He was standing in the middle of the bridge, with his head down. I couldn't see his face, but he was holding up something that looked like a gold watch on a chain, swinging it back and forth, like he was trying to hypnotize someone. I slammed on my breaks, but the road was slick, and I ended up in the river. I assumed I was dreaming, but I'm not sure."

"Calvin, be careful! I don't think you're alone out here!" he shouted.

He was running backward as he took the quilt off. "I will lay your quilt here. Bye, Calvin. There is no way I can ever thank you enough for saving my life! Take care of yourself. Happy birthday, and Merry Christmas!" He turned around and stumbled onto the road.

Calvin heard a pair of old worn-out breaks come to a squeaking halt, then a door slam. He listened as the rumbling noise of the old truck slowly disappeared.

Calvin's heart was pounding. He could barely breathe as he reached inside the cart and opened the cigar box. The watch was gone!

He was sick to his stomach as he dropped to the cold wet ground. Calvin put his head in his hands, and for the second time in his life, he sobbed.

Why would the Canein' Man steal his watch? He had offered it to him for Truman, and he wouldn't take it. This was the last and final blow. It was too much.

The old man driving the equally old truck asked, "Where's yuh shoes?"

"It's kind of a long story. How far to Tallulah?" asked Mr. Clark.

The old man was looking him over. "'Bout eighteen miles to Tallulah. It don't seem right ta pick up folks on Christmas Eve. Yuh thu second one in thu last five minutes."

Hudson Clark turned and tried to look through the back window, but because of the wood frames around the truck bed, he couldn't see anyone.

"There's an ol' feller in da back. Thought at first he wuz uh bear. There's uh bunch around here, yuh know. Yeah, he wuz just sittin' by thu ditch, uh ways back. Had his head down, all bundled up with uh coat an' hat. I thought he wuz asleep or sumt'n, but he stuck his thumb up, so I stopped, an' he jumped in thu back. You'd think folks already got where they needed ta be by now, it bein' Christmas Eve an' all," the old man said as he looked Hudson over again.

Mr. Clark was still trying to see through the wood frames, blocking the view through the back window, but to no avail.

"What did he look like?"

"Didn't get uh good look, but he's wearin' all black, with white gloves. I thought that was odd," said the old man.

"Hum, yes, that is rather strange. Did he tell you where he's going?" asked Mr. Clark.

"He said let 'im off at thu Smith's store."

"Do they have a telephone there?" asked Mr. Clark.

"Shore they do. Just tell Mattie Smith yuh need ta use thu telephone. She won't mind."

The old man was dying to ask him who he was going to call and, while he was at it, ask what happened to his shoes and coat.

"Is the store this side of Tallulah?" asked Clark.

The old guy nodded yes.

"Then I'll get out at the Smith store too," said Mr. Clark.

Hudson had dosed off but opened his eyes when the old truck's tires hit a hole and rocked to a stop for just a moment, as he shifted into low and bounced onto the wooden bridge. As they slowly rumbled across, he gazed down the swift muddy water of the Tensas and relived the horrific way the morning had started.

He thought about his brush with death, and had it not been for the boy and his dog, he would have perished in the river.

He thought about how the boy recounted his amazing survival story without thinking how incredible it must have sounded to someone else.

The water was up, but nothing like the big flood that Calvin had survived. The Tensas had gotten over this very bridge. It would have been hard for anyone to believe an eleven-year-old was capable of doing the things he did, but Hudson Clark was a believer after all he had witnessed this morning.

The river was swollen but still within its banks. There were logs caught high up in trees, six or eight feet above what the water level was now.

The old man saw him looking at the river.

"Yeah, we shore lucky this old bridge's still here. They had ta replace uh few planks an' reinforce thu pilin', but it didn't wash downriver. That's thu main thang, I reckon," said the old fella.

"Mister, I hate ta be nosey, but I just got ta ask, what happened ta yur shoes, an' what were yuh doin' out there in them woods without no coat?"

Hudson was just going to ignore the question. Thankfully, he saw the little clapboard store nestled under the tall oaks.

"It's a long story. I'll tell you about it next time we get together," he said.

The old man frowned and wrinkled his brow. He knew the young man was saying it's none of your business. Being agitated, he applied the brakes a tad too hard. Hudson braced himself against the dashboard as the old truck slid a little in the loose gravel in front of the Smith store.

Hudson reached in his back pocket, took out his wallet, and handed the old man a ten-dollar bill.

"Here, my friend, I thank you so very much, and have a Merry Christmas."

Before the old man had time to respond, Hudson jumped out, slammed the door, and ran to the back of the truck. There was nothing in the bed but a tow sack full of sweet potatoes. He gingerly walked barefooted on the gravel, mixed with sharp soda bottle caps to the driver's side of the truck.

"There's nobody back there!" exclaimed Hudson Clark.

"You don't say. That ol' rascal must've jumped out when I hit dat hole at thu foot of thu bridge. Just don't make no sense. I didn't see 'im get out, and he didn't even say much obliged or nutin'. He didn't git my taters, did he? My wife's gone 'a make me uh pie for Christmas," he said.

"Your sweet potatoes are still there," said Mr. Clark.

"Well, dat's mighty nice, an' I sho do thank yuh for thu ten-dollar bill." Then under his breath, he said, "Even tho it's wet."

Chapter 24

Glory Be

Mr. Clark never looked back; he was almost to the steps, just waved and slipped inside the screen door.

"Anybody here?" he shouted.

"Be right out," a vintage female voice hollered from the back.

"Do you have a telephone I can use?" he asked as he scanned the place looking for one.

"Just hold on. I'm coming. I was 'bout to lock thu back door. I'm closing, for heaven's sake. Don't anybody know it's Christmas Eve? Otis is gone ta thu house. I've been trying ta close for thu last half hour."

A pleasantly plump gray-haired lady popped from behind the curtains to the front counter. She went straight to the shelf under the cash register, never looked up until she firmly set the telephone on top of the counter.

"Here," she said, looking at him for the first time. "Hum, you don't live around here, do yuh?" said Mattie Smith.

"No, ma'am, I live over in Vicksburg. I had a little problem early this morning with my car. I need to call my office and have someone come and get me. I'm Hudson Clark. I have a timber business and sawmill this side of Vicksburg. It'll take about an hour for someone to pick me up, but I will sit out on the porch bench. First, I need to telephone my wife to let her know I'm okay and call my office. You can close and start enjoying Christmas Eve with your husband," said Mr. Clark.

"Don't yuh make no never mind 'bout that. I'll call Otis an' stay here until someone comes ta get 'cha," said Mrs. Smith.

After speaking with his wife, Mr. Clark hung the receiver up and, with wet eyes and a trembling voice, said, "Thank you so much, Mrs. Smith. My wife was a little upset. It's just the two of us, and we were going to have a quiet Christmas alone. I had to explain why I need a ride home. It's been a horrific day, and I'm a lucky man to be alive. Only for the grace of God and a young boy and his dog am I even standing here."

"Come on over by thu stove. I'll add more wood. Your feet are purple from thu cold. Now you just sit down and put yuh feet close to thu fire, an' I'll get yuh a cup of coffee," she said.

"Thanks again for your kindness. Did you possibly know the young boy from Tallulah that people say went missing in the Tensas swamp?" asked Mr. Clark.

"If yuh talking 'bout Calvin Young, absolutely I did! I know just about everybody in these parts. He used ta come in here with other kids from thu Pooles' foster home. I knew him well. Most folks think he's dead. There have been rumors of sightings, but that was before thu big flood," she said, shaking her head.

Calvin was completely drained of any energy and emotion. It didn't make sense to him that the Canein' Man would take his watch. He just wanted to disappear. He wished he could simply dissolve into the black delta soil. It would probably be best for him and everyone else.

Truman had waited patiently for Calvin to get up, but suddenly on his own, he began pulling the cart toward the road. Penny stopped pecking around and hopped on his back. Calvin was num. He just stayed on his knees and watched as the cart was pulled across the ditch and onto the road. He had lost the will or ability to know what to do next.

The cart sat motionless in the middle of the road for a considerable amount of time, then, ever so slowly, took a right turn.

Tears welled up in Calvin's eyes as he said, "Its' over."

Truman didn't move until a shaken Calvin Young slowly walked into his peripheral view. The troop methodically continued in the direction of the old Smith store.

Calvin was oblivious to the image they must have presented to the outside world. The small horse of a dog with a bantam chicken on his head, pulling a miniature covered wagon, tended by a boy with a spear wearing a canvas cloak with a raccoon collar.

Calvin's hair was down to his shoulders. He was wearing the necklace made with boar and gator teeth. The cart was adorned with pots and pans. Hanging off one side was a large smoked buffalo fish.

Calvin had no explanation why he left so many things at the last campsite. These included the fish traps, the net, his bow, and a couple of pots. He even walked past his precious quilt and didn't bother to pick it up. Now, after having his watch taken by the Canein' Man, nothing really mattered or made sense to him anymore. They walked along in silence.

The same old truck that had picked up Mr. Clark now slowly approached the caravan. The driver had already rolled his window down before coming to a complete stop. He stuck his head out the window and shouted, "Hi-de-do there, young feller!"

Truman never slowed his pace, and Calvin refused to make eye contact with the old man.

He put the truck in reverse and managed to stay even with the cart while trying to engage in conversation. Calvin was aware of all the questions the old man was asking, but he just wasn't in the mood to talk.

Finally, the brakes squealed again, and the truck stopped with a little grinding of gears as it was shifted from reverse to low.

The old man just scratched his bald head. "Dis has been thu craziest Christmas Eve I can remember," he said to himself, then drove off.

Calvin knew the cat was now out of the bag. His return happened so fast, and he hadn't prepared for it. He was pretty sure there were a lot of people upset with him, including the sheriff and Mrs. Poole.

He desperately wanted to see Emily Mae again but only without causing her a problem with her new parents. He was assuming she was adopted by now, but until he spoke with Mrs. Poole, he wouldn't know for sure.

Calvin hoped no one else would try to talk to him before they could make it to the store. But he knew there were several sharecropper houses a few miles ahead. He could see smoke rising from a stovepipe sticking through a rusty tin roof. He was about a half mile away, when he heard a dog bark and then several more.

Truman didn't flinch; only the hair stood up on his back. He tightened into a defensive attitude. Calvin had seen him do this before. His body contracted into solid muscle.

"It's okay, boy. Just don't pay them no mind. They're all bark an' no bite," Calvin said quietly as he rubbed his back.

He knew now that every dog from here to Tallulah would know they were coming, and that meant every person who owned the dogs also knew.

He hadn't prepared mentally for this. Everything just happened. It started from the moment he was awakened by someone hollering, "Help!" When he realized his watch had been taken, everything seemed to be beyond his control. Truman had made the decision for him to return, and now it was too late to turn back.

As they approached the gray unpainted house, dogs were waiting at the edge of the dirt driveway. They were making themselves as tall as possible, prancing back and forth, hair raised on their backs. Some were barking hysterically, and others were growling menacingly with a low guttural sound.

The screen door to the old house flew open. A stout black woman holding a baby on her hip came out on the porch and began shouting at the dogs.

"Shut up with all dat racket, an' git away from dat big dog befo yuh make him mad!"

It didn't take much for the mutts to change their tune once they got a good look at Truman.

Four other children, from about three to eight years old, came running right up to Calvin. They just stood looking at him as though he was an attraction at a carnival. Calvin felt his face turning a deep shade of red as they surrounded the weary travelers.

They were in a jubilant mood, laughing, touching everything including Calvin and Truman. Miss Penny politely moved just enough to keep the little fingers from poking her.

The woman with the baby on her hip, stepped off the porch, and hollered, "Yo young'uns, git away fum dat big ol' dog! Do he bite?"

By then the children were already hugging and petting Truman. Calvin could tell he was a little uncomfortable but tolerated it just the same.

A little boy pulled the raccoon tail on Calvin's cloak collar and said, "Momma, he's uh Indian. He's wearin' moccasins an' got uh spear."

"Yawl leave dat boy alone," she said as she approached Calvin. She was as curious as the kids.

"Yuh him, ain't yuh? Yuh dat wild boy, thu one dat lives down in de bottom, ain't yuh?" she said. "How come yuh come out 'uh de swamp? Are yuh goin' back ta yo homeplace?"

She stopped talking to Calvin long enough to holler, "Yuh better git back befo dat dog eats yuh up. I'm not gone 'a tell yuh no more."

The oldest little girl hugged Truman even tighter as she said, "No, Momma, he won't bite me. He loves everybody. See, he wants me ta pet 'im."

She then jumped up and ran into the house. Moments later, she came running down the steps with three cookies. With a big smile, she handed them to Calvin and said, "Here's one fer yuh, an' one fer yo big dog an' li'l hen."

"Thanks," Calvin said, blushing. He wasn't used to all this attention. He turned to the woman and asked, "Mam, do ya know Preacher Joe, thu fisherman on thu Tensas?"

She looked startled. "How come yuh ask me dat? Do ya knows where he is?"

"No, mam, he's my friend. I stayed with 'im at thu fish camp uh couple of months. Then one morning I got up, an' he was gone. I looked for 'im, but I couldn't find 'im. I was hopin' yuh could tell me where he is."

The lady's demeanor changed. "No, I'm sorry. I don't know. Nobody knows whar he is. We's 'fraid some'in' happened ta 'im."

"He's my momma's uncle, my great uncle," she said. "I got uh brother dat lives over in Tallulah. He ask de sheriff ta go git 'im 'cause he's too ol' ta be out in da swamp by his self. They's looked for 'im, but nobody's seen 'im fo mo than uh couple uf months."

"Well, I think his daughter was gone 'a have thu sheriff come get 'im so she could take 'im somewhere up north to live with her. I don't think he wanted to leave the river, though," said Calvin.

The woman looked confused. "What daughter? De only daughter he had wuz my momma's aunt. She died 'bout five years ago."

"So he didn't have uh daughter living up north?"

"Not anymore. She wuz seventy-eight when she died. She couldn't take care uf herself, much less him."

"Seventy-eight, yuh mean his daughter was that old? How old is he?"

"Nobody knowed fo' sho'. Some says close ta uh hundred."

"Uh hundred? Me an' him fished thu river ever' day. He's strong, an' he could walk that swamp, good as anybody I know."

"Well, I speck yuh right, but we's all got ta go sometime. I thinks he wuz uh little mixed up in thu' head sometimes he thought Aunt Eller wuz still here. It wuz kind 'a pitiful ta talk ta 'im."

"I know," said Calvin. "I think he went ta see his wife. That's what I think. It was all he talked about."

With watering eyes, through the gray mist, Calvin scanned the swamp, which had been home for him and the preacher. The tall cypress hugging the riverbanks stood high above the thick undergrowth. It recreated the unmistakable dark snakelike outline of the Tensas.

A faint smile crossed his lips as he shook his head. Brother Joe was maybe a hundred years old. It had to be all that laughing he done, thought Calvin.

"I guess I shouldn't worry 'bout him no more. Let's go, Truman."

The little caravan began moving forward. The kids singing Christmas carols escorted them. Even the dogs followed. This continued until their momma called out.

"Yo young'uns better git back here. Yawl gone 'ah miss Christmas. When ya daddy gits back fum de fields, Santa Claus might come." The kids stopped on a dime.

Calvin turned and waved, but they were already running up the steps to the little unpainted house. The three sojourners were alone again.

Mrs. Smith listened quietly to Hudson Clark as he related the extraordinary events of the day. Having shared his experience with his wife and now with Mrs. Smith, he was emotionally drained.

Mattie got up to answer the telephone but stopped and put a hand on his shoulder. "Hudson Clark, thu Lord has more for yuh ta do. That's why you're still here. Your work isn't finished," she said.

"Hello, well, howdy there, Douglas. No, I'm not good 'bout guessing stuff. Just tell me. Glory be! Yuh don't mean it. Where'd yuh see 'im? I'll let thu sheriff know an' uh few other folks. Thanks! Merry Christmas ta you an' thu misses."

Mr. Clark had heard only this end of the conversation and was standing with his back to the woodstove, waiting for Mattie to fill in the blanks.

She hung up the telephone and looked at Hudson for a moment as though trying to process what she had just heard.

"That was old man Douglas Branch, thu fella that dropped yuh off here. You're not goin' to believe this. He went on ta Tallulah but, on thu way back home, saw Calvin Young and uh huge dog pulling uh cart. They were headin' this way."

At that moment, Hudson heard a car pull in and looked out the window. "I've got to go," he said as he grabbed Mattie and gave her a big hug and a kiss on the cheek.

"That's wonderful! It truly is going to be a Merry Christmas, Mattie!" He ran for the door.

"Wait, you're goin' ta catch thu flu, barefooted an' all. At least put this on." Mattie came running after him with an overcoat.

"I think I know who left this on the back steps, along with a bucket of pecans. I picked it up 'cause I didn't want it to get wet if it rained. He won't mind. You can drop it off next time yuh pass this way," she said, draping it over his shoulders as he climbed in on the passenger's side.

"Thanks again, Mattie. You're an angel. My wife and I will see you again soon."

Mattie watched as the car pulled onto the road and quickly disappeared.

"Otis won't believe what I have ta tell him. I think Hudson Clark is right. It is going to be a wonderful Christmas," she said to herself.

Chapter 25

Christmas Day

All was quiet. Nothing made a sound but the crunch of the gravel underfoot as they walked. There were no other automobiles that afternoon. Everyone was with their families enjoying Christmas Eve. Calvin tried desperately to remember the one Christmas with both his parents before his father went off to war.

He often tried to relive it in his mind, but as the years passed, the images were fading.

Calvin wasn't sure what was actual or contrived, but the one memory he would never forget was the way his mother smelled as she held him on her lap while he opened his only present.

His dad gave him a little red plastic tractor. It was the first toy he could remember made of this strange material. The tractor had an odd smell, but his mother smelled wonderful. She smelled like Christmas, everything good, a mixture of pine needles and fresh baked cookies.

Calvin snapped out of his daydream. He actually had cookies in his hand. Maybe that was what he smelled. He had planned to eat them when they got to the bridge.

It was now late Christmas Eve afternoon. The sky lay heavy, and Calvin felt as if he could reach up and touch it. The moisture enveloped them like a wet blanket.

He could smell the river long before getting to the bridge. Emotions of seeing the old bridge after all he had experienced were overwhelming. The Calvin Young who walked across the weathered boards ten months ago didn't exist anymore.

Truman sidestepped a deep hole at the foot of the bridge that washed out during the flood, then pulled the cart to the halfway point. From there, they could see up and down the river. The magnificent cypress was now stripped bare by the winter frost. Their limbs were like dark boney fingers, silhouetted against the gray sky.

Calvin took their cookies, broke them into smaller pieces, and put them on his plate. He unhitched Truman, and they sat on the edge of the bridge with their treat. Calvin dangled his legs over the side as they enjoyed each other's company and celebrated Christmas Eve.

There were fireworks cracking in the distance. A Roman candle of many colors arched across the sky just above the tree line. Then there was silence.

Christmas always made him a little sad inside, knowing that most kids were celebrating with their families. He and Emily Mae had never really had one. Now he hoped she was sitting around a Christmas tree with her new momma and daddy.

His eyes followed the banks of the old Tensas until it melted into the heavy fog. It was part of him now. From the start, he knew it wasn't possible for it to last forever; he knew nothing ever really did. Now he was saying good-bye to two old friends: Brother Joe and the Tensas.

He noticed that the log where he had hung his overall strap was gone. It washed down the river with the flood. That was pretty clever, he thought. Calvin could barely see the top of the giant cypress towering above the others. It was there that he had caught the big forty-pound Appaloosa catfish.

Truman whimpered a little as he stretched out beside him and placed his huge head in his lap. Calvin hugged him. They were leaving their sanctuary. Both were heavy-hearted and unsure of what their future would be.

"Don't worry, boy. Everything's gone uh be all right," Calvin whispered without any certainty.

The stillness was only broken when a couple of wood ducks squealed as they flew overhead to roost. They banked and dropped into a small duckweed-covered slough just off the edge of the river.

Calvin never tired of watching waterfowl with their relentless wingbeat. He thought ducks flew with such urgency, as if they were always late for a meeting, darting here and there, not quite sure where it was being held.

The cookies the little girl had given them were all gone, but Penny was still picking at a couple of crumbs on the metal plate.

It was now time to move on. There was just enough light left to get to the store and gather some pecans before dark. He was looking forward to him and Penny having pecan pancakes. Truman would have the last smoked buffalo fish. They would spend their last night as vagabonds at the very spot where it all started.

Calvin stood and walked to the other side of the bridge. Like a javelin thrower, he made a running start and threw his spear high and deep into the mist. It barely made a sound as it struck the water, and the river sucked it up quickly, taking it downstream.

Truman had a confused look. He wasn't sure if he should try to retrieve it or what. "It's okay, boy. This is where I got it, an' I'm giving it back. Grown-ups wouldn't like me walking 'round with uh sharp object. Anyway that's all it would be to 'em. They're always cautioning us kids how dangerous things are and how we should be careful with sharp objects. Thu most important thing uh kid should never do is run with uh pair of scissors." Calvin smiled.

This was all going over Truman's rather elevated head, and he was still confused.

Then there it was; he could barely make out the outline of the old store in the dark mist. Calvin immediately thought of the Canein' Man. Why would he take his watch? He had already offered it to him for Truman, and he had refused, saying, no, the dog was not for sale or trade; it was a gift. Calvin recalled for the first time the Canein' Man's reaction when he handed him the watch. He seemed to get very emotional about it, as if he knew the name on the back. He wondered why. Nothing made any sense! Calvin just couldn't reconcile the most gut-wrenching thing that had ever happened to him. Why would the Canein' Man give him Truman but steal his watch?

Even though it was only a quarter-mile walk to the store, the sun had already set when they arrived. Calvin was disappointed; now he wouldn't be able to find pecans on the dark ground. He had looked forward to having pecan pancakes.

He was in a melancholy mood as he unhitched Truman. Then he noticed a bucket of pecans sitting on the back steps. This was curious, because why would anyone go to the trouble to gather a bucket of pecans, then leave them on the steps? Perhaps Mrs. Smith planned to make a pecan pie and just forgot them. Regardless, he was thankful and hoped she wouldn't mind if he and Penny had some for supper.

He made a small fire behind the store, near the shed, and began to prepare the meal. Calvin feared for his companions, as they huddled around the small fire. He knew this might be the last time they would be together. Once he showed up at the Pooles' foster home, he would be considered just a boy. Grown-ups would decide what their future would be.

Calvin took a handful of the pecans he had shelled and put them in his bowl. He emptied the last of the flour on top and added a cup of water to the mixture along with one of Penny's eggs. He poured a pancake as large as his skillet. It was symbolic that he used the last spoonful of lard and noticed there was just enough of Brother Joe's honey left in the jar for the pancake.

Everything was coming to an end. Truman was finally going to eat his last smoked fish, and Calvin was sharing the last pancake with his companions.

He remembered an old picture at Midway Baptist Church of the "Last Supper." Jesus shared food with his disciples before facing Pontius Pilate. He felt guilty for even thinking of the comparison. He knew tomorrow wasn't going to be pleasant, but he was pretty sure he wasn't going to be crucified.

They ate their last meal together; then Calvin crawled into the cart and tried to sleep. It was a restless night. He tossed and turned, dreading what tomorrow would bring.

Calvin woke up anxious and with a knot in his stomach. Peeking out the back of the cart, he watched as the sky slowly turned from a dark blue to a pale pink. The day would be clear and cold. The fire was now just a pile of gray ashes.

It was Christmas Day. This was not a good time to come straggling back after causing so much worry and trouble for so many people. Everything happened so fast. He certainly hadn't intended to return on Christmas Day! Now he wasn't prepared to face those he had caused so much concern. He had a feeling the sheriff may have a few choice words for him or perhaps something worse.

Calvin suddenly became very aware of his appearance. There was little he could do now, except groom himself best he could. He found an old washtub in the shed. He rekindled the fire and placed the tub near the fire. He pumped water from the well and poured bucket after bucket until the tub was full. Once the water was heated, Calvin quickly jumped in using his lava soap to lather up from head to toe.

The cold air caused clouds of steam to rise from the tub. Truman seemed amused by the boy sitting in his small sauna, surrounded by plumes of steam.

After bathing, Calvin combed his shoulder-length hair with his fingers and let it air dry. He dressed in his khaki shirt and too-tight khaki pants and then put on the canvas cloak with the raccoon collar. For the final touch, he placed his trophy necklace around his neck. Now it was Truman's turn.

He managed to get only half of the big brute in the tub at a time. Truman seemed to enjoy the warm water and the thorough scrubbing. Calvin marveled at his good condition after all they had been through. The scars on his legs were completely gone. The only real imperfection was the tiny hole in his left ear. He was resigned to the fact he would never know how or why it was there or how the braided lanyard came to be around his neck.

Calvin decided Truman should wear his lanyard. It was like they both were wearing a gold medal signifying their great adventure, an adventure like no other.

It was now time to accept the consequences of his actions. He knew there would be no one out on Christmas morning. The three-mile trip to the Pooles' place should be uneventful.

Calvin's legs became like rubber when he saw the turn off and the old tin roof of the foster home. He could see the very window he climbed out of and dropped to the ground. There were gray puffs of smoke coming from the chimney.

"At least someone is there," he mumbled to himself.

As they reached the long driveway, he stopped in his tracks! A horrible feeling came over him. Something bad must have happened. There were automobiles, and people lined up on both sides of the road. It was Christmas morning. He couldn't imagine why all these people would be here. He wanted to disappear, but it was too late.

Suddenly, a few small dogs began yelping as they ran toward him. Then he heard people cheering; kids began popping firecrackers! Through it all, he saw a little blond-haired girl running with her arms opened wide. Her head thrown back, tears were streaming down her cheeks as she ran like the wind, shouting, "Calvin, you're back! I knew yuh would come back for me!"

Calvin ran ahead of the cart and scooped her up. She buried her wet face against his neck, pulled back to stare at him, and said, "I like yuh coat! That fur collar tickles my nose!

"Calvin, yuh won't believe what's happened," she whispered in his ear. "Mr. Clark, thu man yuh saved an' his pretty wife want 'ta adopt us."

Before Calvin had time to respond, people were gathering around them. The sheriff stuck his hand through the crowd of people and said, "Young man, welcome home! I just want uh shake yuh hand. It's hard ta believe yuh survived thu flood. Everyone thought yuh was uh goner for sure."

Otis and Mattie Smith were there to welcome him home. They tried to give him a hug, but before they could, a tall man with a pen and pad, wearing a cap with the word *PRESS* on it, reached over them and tapped Calvin's shoulder.

"Excuse me, Calvin. I'm from the *Monroe Morning World*. I would like to interview you for the paper, when we have a chance to talk, of course."

Emily Mae was holding him so tight around the neck it was hard for Calvin to respond to everyone trying to talk to him. He lost sight of Truman, so he turned and whistled for him.

Penny and the big dog were being mobbed by dozens of people. An older man took hold of Truman's harness and helped escort him through the crowd. Calvin thanked him and the man nodded.

"My pleasure. It's an honor to meet you. I too have a love for the great Tensas River Bottom and its inhabitants. I truly admire what you have accomplished and would like to write a story about your adventure with your companions. I understand your birthday was Christmas Eve. It's also mine. I'm a wildlife artist, and I do a little writing. Hope you will share your story with me sometime."

People began to step aside as a young man in a black overcoat and his beautiful wife stepped forward. He offered Calvin his hand.

"I would be pleased to introduce you to my wife, Calvin. This is Charlotte. Charlotte, this is Calvin and his wonderful dog, Truman. They saved my life."

Emily Mae loosened her grip on Calvin's neck, slid to the ground, and let Charlotte Clark take her hand.

Mr. Clark continued, "Oh, and this is Miss Penny. She has the best-tasting eggs in the country."

Penny was nervous. She sidestepped from one end of Truman's back to the other, not allowing anyone to touch her. But she never left her perch.

"What a pretty little hen," said Mrs. Clark, smiling as she rubbed and patted Truman's large head.

While choking back tears, she bent over and hugged and kissed Calvin on the cheek.

"Thank you with all my heart."

Calvin thought she smelled like Christmas: everything good, a mixture of pine needles and fresh baked cookies.

Mr. Clark began to speak to Calvin. "Calvin, we want you and Emily Mae to come live with us if that's something you would like to do. Mrs. Poole's health is failing her. She wanted to be here but couldn't. She has gone to live with her sister. Her hope was something like this might happen. Emily Mae refused to be adopted, because she knew you would return for her someday."

"Oh, by the way, I have something I think might belong to you."

Mr. Clark reached into the black overcoat pocket and took out a gold watch on a chain. He placed it in the boy's hand.

Calvin slowly rubbed the surface, then turned it over. Something was different. The name "Hawk Young" had been scratched through and below it was written "*YOUNG HAWK.*"

The End

Credits

Reference: Holt Collier
Southern Memorie
True Stories from The American South
By Judd Hambrick 2011

Reference: Quaker Story
Jonathan Dickinson's Journal, or God's
Protecting Providence
By John Dickinson 1696
Published By Florida Classic Library 1961

Reference: Frisby House
By Sam Hanna
Staff Writer, Monroe Morning World 1957
Death of Norman Frisby
Frisby Family Version
Flowers Family Version
Mose Martin's Version

About the Author

Ronnie Wells has been a naturalist, as well as a wildlife artist, for over forty years. He grew up in North Louisiana and had grandparents who owned a grocery/gas station outside of Tallulah that he had visited often. Over the years, he came to know and love the Tensas River Bottom.

Ronnie Wells is known nationally as a wildlife artist, both painter and sculptor. One of his monumental sculptures stands in front of the National Headquarters of Ducks Unlimited in Memphis, Tennessee.

Ronnie Wells also wrote and illustrated the children's book, *The Legend of Catfish and Little Bream*, first published by Acadian House Publishing Company in Lafayette, Louisiana.